THE MAGIC

CAROLYN HECTOR

HARLEQUIN® KIMANI™ ROMANCE

Recycling programs
for this product may
not exist in your area.

ISBN-13: 978-0-373-86430-0

The Magic of Mistletoe

Copyright © 2015 by Carolyn Hall

For questions and comments about the quality of this book please contact us
at CustomerService@Harlequin.com.

HARLEQUIN®
™ www.Harlequin.com

Printed in U.S.A.

Having your story read out loud as a teen by your brother in Julia Child's voice might scar some folks from ever sharing their work. But **Carolyn Hector** rose above her fear. She currently resides in Tallahassee, Florida, where there is never a dull moment. School functions, politics, football, Southern charm and sizzling heat help fuel her knack for putting a romantic spin on everything she comes across. Find out what she's up to on Twitter, @Carolyn32303.

Books by Carolyn Hector

Harlequin Kimani Romance

The Magic of Mistletoe

Visit the Author Profile page at
Harlequin.com for more titles

I would like to dedicate this book first and foremost
to my husband and two kids.
Thank you for allowing me the time to write.
And to the Hotties of The Color of Love Book Club.

Acknowledgments

I have to acknowledge Scott Kopel, Janet Atwater-Manuel,
David Dickerson, Rhea Lathan and Aron Myers,
who stormed into my office and demanded I strum up
the courage to hit the submit button.

Chapter 1

"Hold still, I've almost got it." Macy Cuomo parted her thirteen-year-old daughter's hair down the center. As Gia sat at on a stool in front of the vanity in the downstairs bathroom of their two-story home, Macy stood behind her, working the comb through her hair. The door remained open to get rid of the heat from the curling irons, flat irons and hot combs all plugged into the wall.

"Jeez, Mom, why can't you just send me to the hairdresser's to get a blowout like Talia's mom does for her?"

Talia's mom, Jaime Jones, had an ex-husband who made child support payments on time. She also spent more time with a bottle of wine than she did with her own children. Those were some of the reasons why

Macy wasn't going to follow anything that Jaime did for her daughter. "Oh, but think of all the bonding time we get." Macy offered a wide, sweet smile as she slid the flat iron down to the end of Gia's long dark hair.

Finally Gia sat still. With her oldest quiet, Macy concentrated on fixing her hair. The music for the local Tallahassee morning news show filtered through the air. Macy's eight-year-old son, MJ, had sprawled his little body out on the living room floor and was tossing his baseball up in the air.

"Oh, MJ, turn that up!" Gia yelled, craning her neck to peer into the living room.

"Hold still!" Macy said again.

"Mama, it's Duke Rodriguez!"

Duke!

She needn't be reminded who the man was. Every weekday morning for the past two weeks, the flat-screen television mounted on the wall had remained on the news station. The guest host of the local morning show, Duke Rodriguez, united the three of them for various reasons. MJ made up his part of the fan club because of Duke's history as a professional baseball player. Gia, the budding media queen, followed the sports-figure-turned-news-anchor for his ability to merge politics with social events of the world in his broadcasts. As for Macy, she adored him for the main reasons every red-blooded woman did—the man was hot. Macy's stomach fluttered with butterflies every time his deep voice entered the room. Not that she'd ever act on it. He was a celebrity, for God's sake. Not to mention she had no time for a man in her life.

Duke's baritone laugh emanated from the television in the living room and drifted down the hall. Macy leaned out of the doorway to get a better look at the dreamy man.

"Mario Junior, do not stand so close to the TV," Macy yelled as she pulled the comb through the roots of Gia's hair.

"Aw, Mom!" whined MJ as he stepped backward to the oversize brown leather couch, nearly tripping over his white tennis shoes on the way.

"Just do it. And put your shoes on!" Macy glanced at the cell phone in Gia's hand. The minute Gia realized her mother was looking, she held the phone against her chest. Macy rolled her eyes toward the ceiling, not understanding how Gia could get so offended over her privacy when she posted every emotion, feeling and thought on Twitter.

"But Mama!" MJ petitioned loudly.

A lot of mothers could only envision what their children were going to be when they got older. Macy was positive MJ was going to be a lawyer. He loved to argue, and by the early age of four had always come up with good cases. But today he was going to lose. Macy was in no mood. She was already running behind schedule and should have been walking out of the house right about now. She had several errands to run before she had to get to the storage center and start pulling out her equipment.

"They're just about to get to the Santa story. Remember, we saw him last week!"

"I want to see!" Gia said, scrambling from the chair

the minute Macy set the flat iron on the edge of the sink. She clicked the button off and turned off all the other salon-style hair equipment, then followed Gia into the cluttered living room. Yet another thing Macy knew she was going to have to do at some point today before Mario came over to pick up the kids. Her ex-husband would surely tease her if he saw the mess, especially considering that had been one of her complaints about him during their divorce.

Macy leaned against the arm of the couch and pushed the long sleeves of her thin blue shirt up to her elbows. She crossed one leg over the other and realized she needed to put on her shoes, too. Quickly running upstairs to her bedroom, she grabbed a pair of braided flip-flops. Typically she didn't wear flip-flops with jeans, but today she had so much to do that they were convenient. Besides, the late November weather was still warm and balmy. She made it back to the living room in time to hear her daughter sighing. What a way to start a chaotic Monday morning. One more half day of school, and the kids would be out for Thanksgiving break.

"Duke!" Gia gasped, all lovesick. Macy could have sworn her moody teenager even batted her eyelashes at the television screen.

"And I bet the local high school baseball coach is going to ask for his old job back." Duke chuckled. As the family all gathered in the living room, the high definition of the television captured the cheeks of Duke's cohost turning a bright shade of pink, as they had every day since he came to WKSS.

"Speaking of Santa, we're expecting a sighting."

Juliette Walker twirled her hair around her finger and blinked flirtatiously at Duke. Obviously the young co-host was as smitten with Duke Rodriguez as Macy.

This morning, he wore a well-tailored black suit, crisp white Oxford shirt and a red tie. Without acknowledging Juliette's attempt to flirt, Duke shuffled the papers together in front of him in his large hands; a megawatt smile tugged at his square jawline, involuntarily exposing his dimples. Even after being away from sports for ten years, Duke still maintained a fit frame—broad shoulders and a tapered waist. He kept his straight black hair short and close-cropped. Unlike the typical news anchor, Duke wore a well-trimmed goatee to frame his luscious, full lips. Macy cleared her throat to keep from swaying when Duke blinked his thick lashes.

"Already?" Duke asked.

"Yes, I hear he'll be at the mall this Black Friday morning. Oh, I can recall the days of going to the mall and sitting on Santa's lap. What about you, Duke?"

Duke shuffled his paperwork and nodded his head. "I tried to milk Santa for all that I could."

"No way." Juliette gawked.

"It's true," Duke said with a nod. "But it had to be the right Santa, you know what I mean?" he asked, but didn't give Juliette a chance to reply. "I mean, that Santa I saw setting up down at the mall looks like a total fake. Did you see his beard?"

A sinking feeling washed over Macy at that very moment. She pushed herself off the wall. "Okay, kids, let's finish getting ready…"

"Wait!" Gia exclaimed.

"...to this day, I'm almost tempted to sit on a Santa's lap if he's got a real beard."

"You wouldn't dare!" Juliette said.

"Well, maybe not now. I mean, I tried to let every Santa I saw know what I wanted for Christmas until I was about thirteen. And at that point my mom had to smack me on the head and tell me that Santa isn't..."

The scene before Macy felt as if it moved in slow motion. Macy and Gia both tried to get to the television to turn it off before that damn Duke ruined everything. Gia was singing "Fa la la la la" loudly and running toward MJ to distract him. Macy ran in front of the television, tripping over MJ's shoes in the process before she could turn it off. But it was too late.

"...real."

MJ stood there as his large round brown eyes glistened with the threat of tears. "Did he just say Santa wasn't real?"

When you out Santa as a fraud on public television, there are bound to be some repercussions.

Duke Rodriguez found this out the hard way, especially when the woman whose attention he'd been trying to get wouldn't reciprocate any smile he offered each time their eyes met. The caramel beauty in the cream-colored dress stood under the mistletoe, refusing to return his notorious dimpled grin. Fortunately, his invitation to his boss's annual Thanksgiving dinner had not been rescinded. And he owed that to his mother, Janet Rodriguez, for teaching him to own up to his mistakes and hold his head high.

By coming to the party, he hoped to show the rest of the news team at WKSS, who were present at the studio to drop their children off at the daycare, how sorry he was for outing Santa. He brushed off being subjected to juvenile hostility from his colleagues. He hadn't been pushed out of a food line since kindergarten, yet today one person purposely cut in front of him. Another person had swiped the last fork before he could reach it, and then just as he'd reached for a ladle of eggnog, the woman before him let it slip into the creamy punch bowl, slopping the beverage all over the front of his shirt and suit jacket. He handled it with ease and a tight-lipped smile. The story of him revealing Santa Claus as a fraud would blow over soon enough.

"I feel responsible for not fully explaining how family-oriented our staffers are at *Tune In, Tallahassee*. The station likes to go all out for the children at our day care and some of the children we've had on our spotlight segments. We host a party, trim a tree and I even dress up like Santa. Send me the bill for your dry cleaning."

Duke glanced up from his poor attempt to clean the stain off his white button-down shirt. The autumn-colored napkin he used had begun to shred, leaving orange, yellow, and red paper streaks. "I'm going to hold you to it, Pablo."

Chuckling, Pablo nodded his head. With each bob, Duke caught a glimpse of the beginning signs of the horseshoe-patterned baldness of his thinning hair but decided not to tease him right now. Pablo kept his hair curly and low. Duke usually kept his hair as short as Caesar himself. A lot of people often thought he and Pablo were brothers. They were close to the same height, but Pablo had him by maybe a half an inch. Had Pablo not spent the summer back in the Dominican Republic, they both would have been the same hazelnut shade of brown. While Duke liked to dress in finer clothes, Pablo had always been comfortable in a pair of jeans and a polo shirt. Today he wore a red pullover. Duke guessed it was to announce the upcoming Christmas holiday.

"Whatever," Pablo said. "This is the least I can do for inviting you into the lion's den. I never would have guessed—" Pablo handed Duke another napkin, a white one "—considering what a rock star you were two weeks ago, that you'd go down in flames."

"Thanks," Duke grumbled, taking the napkin from his overdramatic friend. As one of the highest-rated news anchors for Multi-Ethnic Television, someone who never took time away from work, Duke knew his career in journalism was far from endangered. Duke enjoyed working for the Orlando, Florida–based company. Multi-Ethnic Television, with affiliate stations all over the nation, prided themselves on diversity, not only in the news anchors but in their shows, as well. Every sitcom, cooking show, or drama or reality series showcased different nationalities from the Caribbean, Africa, India and everywhere else that made up America's cultural melting pot.

With his contract renewal set to be signed at the beginning of the year, MET checked in with him every other week to verify his happiness. He also figured they wanted to know if their *DC Nightly News* anchor planned on returning to the news desk after he finished covering the morning anchorwoman's period of maternity leave.

But they might be getting their journalist back sooner rather than later. His time in Tallahassee might be limited, thanks to the hordes of soccer moms threatening to change morning shows and local business owners flooding Pablo's email inbox, warning they might remove their holiday ads as long as Duke was on the air. Duke's arrival in Tallahassee earlier this month seemed so long ago.

Just because his best friend was his current station manager didn't mean Duke had gotten off any easier. After shouting at him all morning long, Pablo suggested Duke do some serious investing in PR work if he wanted to help save the ratings. Despite his limited time in town, Duke prided himself on maintaining a positive image.

The anchorwoman he was subbing in for was Pablo's wife and the mother of Duke's three—now four—godchildren, so he was really here more so as a favor. He'd leaped from being a baseball star to being in front of the camera in DC, filling people's homes with current events for the past fifteen years, without missing a beat. Being down here with Pablo and his family, however, made him wonder what things he had missed out on in life. After the New Year, Duke had some serious decisions to make.

Somewhat, a little voice nagged him.

"Oh, and her name is Macy Cuomo," Pablo leaned in and whispered, "in case you were wondering. She's single and a very good friend to Monique and me."

He was wondering. He'd been staring at the petite beauty since she walked in the front doors of the Baez family's home two hours ago. There were no obvious signs of her flirting with anyone else, either. Once she'd laid her manicured hand on a man's chest as she tossed her head back and laughed at something that was said, but that was it. At that moment, Duke would have given anything to be that man.

"What?" Duke tried to shake off his gaze, realizing Pablo was speaking to him.

"Yeah, you look like you need to cool off," Pablo said, pushing something into Duke's hand. "You're sweating from staring at her. Take this."

He looked down to his left and spied the green bottle of beer in Pablo's hands. Frost billowed off the beverage.

"You guys have the heat on as if it were freezing."

"It's sixty-eight degrees outside," Pablo countered with a shake of his head. "You forget our moms bundled us up at seventy degrees in the DR."

"And yet you're wearing *chancletas* with jeans?" Duke chuckled. "I heard Thanksgiving is going to be in the seventies."

"Leave my flip-flops alone." Pablo laughed, lifting his foot. "Anyway, you know that's not what I meant. I'm just glad to see you're back on your feet and looking at a quality woman."

"So I've been staring?" Duke looked back at the angel in cream. Pablo was right; he had been away from the Dominican Republic for a while now. He forgot how much he missed a shapely woman with all the right curves in all the right places. This woman named Macy now stood with Monique, cooing over two-week-old baby Lucia. There was a maternal vibe coming from her that worried him. Most of the women he dated never lasted long if they started cooing over children. Duke could offer a woman jewels, trips, cars and other luxury gifts, but not a baby. A childhood illness had scarred him, prohibiting him from being able to give her a biological child. So why bother leading her on any further?

"Let's just say that you've been staring so much you've got Monique wanting to play matchmaker. If I didn't come over here to get you, I am sure she would have been printing out your wedding invitations."

Matchmaking time, Duke thought with a wicked grin. "That doesn't sound too bad. I think my best-friend-in-law has great taste."

Pablo choked on his beer and looked at him as though he'd grown a second head. "What?"

"I'm serious."

"You didn't say that when she tried setting you up with her college roommate."

The college roommate in question had had a unibrow and a questionable Adam's apple. She was one of the five girls Monique shared a room with. Duke had agreed to go on that date sight unseen. Pablo spent the entire double date apologizing for the misfortune.

The two friends looked at each other, both realizing they had the same image in their minds. "At least this time I can see what I'm getting up front."

"And at least this time I can tell you that she's not like the women you've gone out with, Duke. This one is a nice family girl."

Feigning hurt, Duke clutched his chest. "You wound me."

"Mo will wound you if you hurt her." Pablo slapped his best friend on the back playfully and led him across the room to where the woman in question was.

A few people glared at Duke. And then it dawned on him that the reason why this Macy wouldn't look at him must be because she'd already heard the story of his outing Santa. Through a frozen smile, Duke leaned over to his friend. "So you don't think that this lady heard about my Santa mistake on the morning news, do you?"

"Hell, who do you think was the first person to call me?"

"Ugh," Duke groaned and stopped walking.

Pablo pressed the bottle of beer against Duke's shoulder to push him forward. "Face the music. At least when Macy sees Lucia with her *padrino*, she won't think you're a complete ass."

As godfather to Pablo's first three children, Wellinson, Angel and Maylen, Duke knew that women held a soft spot for men who liked kids. Women blatantly hit on him whenever he took the children out to the park or to a game, slipping him their business cards or hotel key cards.

Growing up in Mao, a city in the Dominican Republic, Duke never realized he was poor. His father, Ramon, would say they were blessed. Christmas traditions were more like a big celebration with fireworks and lots of eating. When he got older and came to the States at eighteen, he realized that other people around the world celebrated completely differently from him. It was all about the commercialization of the season. And when it came to his godchildren, Duke was in sync with everyone else.

Duke fell back into step with Pablo. They crossed the hardwood floors of the living room, ignoring some of the eye-rolling that took place when Duke walked through. In the dining area, they found Monique beaming at the sight of them approaching. She opened her arms for him to hug. Duke reached for her and twirled her around. The tie of her black wrap dress flowed through the air as the curls of her blond hair bounced up and down.

"You look way too good to have just given birth two weeks ago," Duke said. "The both of you look great." He smiled down at baby Lucia. "*Dios lo bendiga.*"

"Oh, Duke, you always know what to say." Monique giggled and batted her blue eyes at him.

Their playful banter always warranted a growl from Pablo. "Don't listen to her," Pablo grumbled miserably. "She passed over my head the minute she found out she was pregnant."

Macy looked up from the baby for a moment. Duke noticed her light brown eyes and felt his breath get caught in his throat. She was breathtakingly beautiful.

"What's that?" she asked.

Duke took the opportunity to explain; hopefully his translation of a Dominican superstition might impress her. "Oh, you see, in the Dominican, if a woman passes over the top of her husband's head, he will get all her morning sickness."

Her perfectly manicured eyebrows came together in confusion. "I still don't understand."

"Most women carry the brunt of the morning sickness. Her body has to pass over his head. I mean, usually this happens when the man is sitting on a step and the woman will swing her leg over his head, like a high kick." Duke winked and held his hand over the top of his head. Did he really wink? He wished he could take it back. She seemed so sophisticated. Did she smell like sweet coconut? Suddenly, his train of thought was lost, and he just stood there staring at her, willing the next words to come out of his mouth.

Saving him, Pablo used his beer hand to nudge Duke once again and pointed toward the front stairs. Duke knew Pablo had had the house built for his wife. The stairs were a grand ordeal, coming right out of the pages of *Gone with the Wind*. "See that sixth step right there?" He looked back at Duke and Macy to make sure they were watching. "I was walking by these steps, minding my own business, when my wife nearly flew from that step onto the floor over the banister right over my head. It was like watching one of those bad seventies movies."

"Hey," Monique laughed, "I was barely eight weeks pregnant and still jogging every morning. but there was no way I could pass up a chance to test out the superstition."

The image made everyone laugh. Duke noticed how Macy was even prettier up close and smiling. The lighting framed her heart-shaped face, highlighting her café-au-lait skin, haloing the top of her light brown curly hair. Because of her flawless skin, he could not determine her age. The news anchors he'd worked with would kill for the illegal lengths of Macy's lashes. Her brown eyes crinkled in the corners as she stared at the three of them, her lips parted. Duke still stared, trying not to be a pervert, but the dangerous curves on her reminded him of the beautiful women back home—thick in the thighs, breasts and behind. His breath caught in his throat again. Asking if she was a model would have been something she'd already heard. She could have been on television. He wondered if she was in the business. He prayed not, because the last thing he wanted was to get involved with another woman in the industry. His last relationship had played out in the gossip tabloids from beginning to end, leaving a bitter taste in his mouth.

A lull fell across the foursome. Seemingly nervously, Monique cleared her throat. "So Duke, are you enjoying yourself? Pablo wanted to make sure you got some of the old Dominican traditions."

"Everything is great. Who made *pasteles en hojas*?"

"Pablo." Monique beamed. It didn't surprise Duke to learn that. The *masa*, or dough, was made up of plantains and other root vegetables. Getting it to the right consistency took a lot of time.

"That's good. It will go great with the bottle of Anis del Mono I had shipped in."

For most people, the anise in the liqueur had a strong flavor like licorice, thus making it an acquired taste. Ready for the strong Spanish liqueur, Duke looked around the room at the traditionally festive holiday atmosphere. Christmas was less than six weeks away, and they'd already had their home decorated in bright red, green and white. The Christmas tree in the family room had to be about seven feet tall and was decorated with matching red and green ornaments.

"The food, the decorations, everything looks great, Mo."

"Well, I can't take all the credit," Monique said.

"No?" Duke could see Macy out of the corner of his eye. She held baby Lucia close to her and with expertise. Despite Duke's status as godfather to all the Baez kids, he still always felt awkward holding one.

Monique hit herself lightly in the head. "Oh my God! Where are my manners? Macy, this is Duke Rodriguez, practically one of the family. Duke, this is our dear friend Macy. She's the one who did all of this." She waved her hand around the room.

"It's a pleasure to meet you," Duke said, extending his hand. Since she was holding the baby with both arms, she couldn't shake. Duke felt a little foolish. Quickly, he shoved his hand in his pocket.

"Nice to meet you." Her words sounded polite, but there was a clip in her voice that told Duke she was just being nice.

Not counting the echoing chuckle as Pablo took a sip from his beer, there was another awkward silence between them. Kenny G's melodic holiday saxophone notes were easily heard as the sound system dispersed the music through the rooms. Forks scraping against plates and champagne glasses being clinked in toast filtered through the air, as well. Monique raised her eyebrow in Duke's direction. He could read it. She'd done her part, and now it was time for him to make an impression. After years of dating, years of having women throw themselves at him, Duke felt something strange; he was at a loss for words.

Macy didn't seem the slightest bit awestruck looking at him. She'd barely glanced up when Monique made the introductions. With one hand in his pocket and one still holding his now-room-temperature beer, Duke stood there, rocking back and forth.

He towered over her by a good half a foot. Up close, he could see that her chocolate-brown hair was highlighted with little streaks of gold. She still wouldn't give him eye contact, but he could see that she had the longest lashes and barely any makeup on her top lids. When she smiled down at baby Lulu, he could see her regal cheekbones rise slightly.

Monique reached over and popped her husband on the arm. "Oh my gosh, I told you not to let me forget the thing."

"Ouch. The what?" Pablo asked, rubbing his arm.

A person had to be blind not to notice how Monique tilted her head toward the kitchen. She was obviously trying to give the two strangers a moment. Macy wasn't blind, but she was clearly devoting all her attention to the baby in her arms. "Macy, will you be a dear and watch Lucia for me for a second?"

"Not a problem," Macy replied sweetly, looking up for a moment.

Even when they were alone, Macy avoided Duke's

eye contact. He wasn't going to leave until she smiled at him. "So you're a caterer?" he guessed.

"I cater to people, but not like you may think."

Her voice was thick, melodic. Maybe she was an aspiring singer. "Well, that's interesting. You know, I just may be in need of your services."

Finally she looked up, but when she did, he truly felt the icy glare of the *mal ojo* she gave him. He shivered. The evil eye told him she wanted nothing at all to do with him. "I'm booked."

"But I didn't say when." He tilted his head down so she could see him give her an award-winning smile. He also didn't give up that easily. If she saw it, it didn't have any effect on her, though.

Macy squared her shoulders and finally gave him a direct stare. Duke could see that her eyes were a golden brown. Her lips made a cute bow, even if they were frowning at him. "I don't need to know, Mr. Rodriguez. I'm pretty booked until the time you're gone."

Duke pressed his lips together to keep from grinning too hard. She knew how long he was going to be in town? That gave him a glimmer of hope she'd been following his time in Tallahassee. "I would pay you double what your normal fee is."

"It doesn't matter what you want to pay," Macy stated again. "I'm extremely busy, and I don't think you understand what exactly it is that I do."

"Okay, okay, maybe we can talk about it over dinner?" Taking a long sip of his beer to figure out what he was going to say next, Duke nodded his head. "Oh wait, I guess you don't like to cook since you do it all the time, right? You, um, did the cooking for tonight, right?" he asked when she gave him a funny look. Her left eye squinted a bit, and her smile was crooked, devilish almost.

"I did the decorating," she clarified.

Duke looked around him, the furniture, the caramel-colored walls with the white trimming, and the fixtures. "Oh, you're an interior decorator."

She smiled, finally. He thought he could leave now, but he was too captivated. Her smile lit up the room. It ignited something within him. Something he hadn't felt in a long time. His mother used to say he was going to fall in love at first sight, but he wasn't quite sure if this was it. All Duke knew was that he did not want to leave this woman's side, even if she was making it obvious that she didn't want to be around him.

"I'm more of an exterior decorator, especially for the holidays."

"This is interesting," Duke replied with a raised eyebrow. Women always fell for that move. Dwayne "The Rock" Johnson had nothing on him. "You mean you painted the house?" She was so dainty and feminine, it wasn't something he expected.

"No." Macy shook her head and huffed. She was obviously growing irritated with him. He'd never had that happen with a woman. Brown curls bounced from side to side, framing her face. "I did the holiday decorations outside."

Duke recalled the Santa, the snowmen and the elves playing outside. It was quite the picturesque scene. There were a few homes in his neighborhood that were putting up their decorations, also. In fact, he'd gotten a letter in the mail about keeping up with the neighborhood traditions. "The decorations are great. Maybe you can do the same at my place."

She half smiled this time, then adjusted Lucia so that she was resting over her shoulder. Duke noticed that her ring finger was naked. "As I've said, I'm busy, Mr. Rodriguez." She tried to move away, but Duke stepped in her way.

"Hey, maybe I can do a story on you. This sounds like a fascinating one."

"Sorry," Macy said. Her snarky half smile told him she could go toe-to-toe with him and with anything he had to offer. "You're obviously new here. A story has been done." She moved to the right, and Duke moved to the left, blocking her once again. She sighed impatiently as she looked at him. The light from the skylight hit across her eyes, turning her eyes a seductive shade of golden brown.

"I feel like you're upset with me."

"Now why would I be upset with you, Mr. Rodriguez?" This time she offered a forced toothy smile, showing her dimple on her right cheek. "We've just met."

She was being sarcastic. He liked that. Women weren't sarcastic enough with him. They pretty much caved to whatever he said.

And then a bomb went off in the pit of his stomach at the ultimate possibility. *Maybe she genuinely just was not attracted to him*. His years of speaking in front of the camera, eloquently, went out the window. He found himself beginning to stutter, "Well, I…"

And then she ambushed him with her reasoning. "Could it be because yesterday morning while I was getting my kids ready and listening to the morning news, you exposed Santa as a fraud in front of my eight-year-old? Do you realize how many mothers had to explain to their children that you're just a pompous ass whom Santa stopped visiting a long time ago and that you're just so bitter that you wanted to ruin Christmas for everyone?"

He winced and snapped his teeth together as she gave him a thorough tongue-lashing. When she quieted down, Duke felt guiltier than ever. Pablo had said she'd been the first to call and complain. How soon he'd forgotten, after being lost in her beauty.

"Oh…" He scratched at the back of his head, still at a loss for words.

A few people within earshot overheard and were snickering, championing Macy.

"I'm real sorry about that. Maybe I can talk to her…"

"Him." She corrected him quickly.

Duke nodded. "I'm very sorry. Can I do anything to fix this situation?"

Once again Macy shook her head from side to side. "I highly doubt it."

"Can I at least take you to dinner sometime? Maybe take your son out for a tour of the studio?"

Macy sighed irritably. He could see that she wasn't a person to make angry. If her eyes could literally shoot daggers, he'd be dead right now. "There is nothing you can say or do. What's done is done, Mr. Rodriguez."

"Duke," he corrected her.

"What?" Macy pulled her neck back in confusion.

"My first name, it's Duke. My friends call me Duke."

"You are such an athle-tante."

"A what?" Duke laughed.

"It means you're like one of those celebrity athletes who think you can say and do whatever you like you're some society debutante." Rolling her eyes, she choked out a haughty laugh, then shook her head no. "I'm not interested. So you have a nice evening, Mr. Rodriguez."

Dumbfounded, Duke stood there and watched her disappear around the corner into the kitchen. If she went through the swinging doors without looking back, then he knew he didn't have a shot at her. His heart slammed against his ribs, a strange reaction he'd never felt before from just meeting a woman for the first time, because when she reached the door, she pushed one side open, stopped and cast a glance over her shoulder, directly at him.

Chapter 2

The day after the party, Macy found herself sitting in her office, thumbing through various sketches she'd worked on all morning. The swivel chair squeaked as she leaned back in a half stretch, half yawn, her eyes surveying the room. In times like these, she still did not believe how blessed she was to have such a successful career. The two-story Victorian office she owned in historic Frenchtown had doubled as the home where she'd raised her children until she earned enough money. Now she traveled in to work from her ranch-style home just outside the city limits.

For ten years, Macy had worked her fingers to the bone, using her skills as an interior decorator for a corporation and moonlighting during the holidays as an exterior decorator to help pad her little nest egg. Oh, how hard the first two years of starting her own business were—she'd been in the middle of a divorce from her best friend at the time, Mario Polizzi, and taking care of an infant and a precocious child.

Macy owed a lot to Mario, and it was easy to maintain their friendship now simply because they both realized they never should have gotten married. Mario and his family had played a big part in Macy's life ever since her parents had passed away. Since they dated exclusively throughout high school, they both figured marriage was their next step. Getting pregnant right after prom sped up their plans. While trying to rebuild her life, Macy took on clients who needed help with their outside decorating ideas for the holidays. That business became a niche in town and led her to become extremely successful.

In a few weeks, all the homes in Tallahassee would be judged for their holiday spirit. Each neighborhood nominated a winner and posted their favorite home on Pinterest. From there, the home with the most votes collected a win. The award, courtesy of the mayor's office, came with a cash prize, but more important, clout in the community for having the most spirit. In the past ten years, one of Macy's homes had always won. Her biggest competitor was herself. But she never took all the credit. Each customer would sit down with her and give their ideas of what they wanted. Macy just put it into motion.

Now here she sat, a successful decorator, and she couldn't focus on one single thing. The Christmas clock down the hall ticked away. The bells on the front door indicating a visitor were silent. In a way, Macy hoped the feeling of excitement when she heard her bells chime over her front door would never go away. It kept her on her toes. There was always a challenge lurking around the corner, but right now she desperately needed some motivation. The Wainwrights' ideas weren't sparking anything with her.

The Wainwrights were her latest clients. They were a middle-aged couple, married for twenty years, and wanted to finally get involved in the Christmas tradition. None of Macy's suggestions had worked for them, and none of theirs were things Macy could pull off. She couldn't make real snow appear and stick for the duration of the holiday season. They had a hard time understanding that if they did not sign their contract, Macy would not to be able to help them. They were going to have to stop just showing up every other day with their latest outrageous ideas.

Tucking her pencil behind her ear, Macy adjusted the cowl-necked sweater and strained her ear for her latest Christmas gadget, a buff, half-naked Santa with one hand on his hip and the other behind his head while he gave off a hearty "ho, ho, ho."

Any distraction was welcome right about now. The lead from her pencil barely made any marks. For the first time in a long time, her mind was elsewhere. Her wrists flicked a few times, sketching the outline of a face that had haunted her all night long. From the curve of his lips to his chiseled jawline, Duke Rodriguez's face was burned into her brain. Two cups of coffee couldn't get her to concentrate. Duke's cocky smile, his eyes and the way he flirted with her yesterday flashed through her mind.

Matters didn't get better when the office timer went off and the television screen popped on, directly to WKSS channel seven. Duke's deep baritone voice filtered through the office. She'd turned her back on the television, but she could still hear him as if he were right behind her. She would never admit it out loud, but his deep voice with the slight island accent made her stomach flip with butterflies. The fact that he had this kind of effect on her bothered her to no end. She was supposed to dislike him. And yet she couldn't stop thinking about him.

There had been a whisper running through the Baez home last night when he'd dared to show his face. Everyone with children who watched *Tune In, Tallahassee*, the morning show, fumed with anger. Macy expected her friends to break out the pitchforks, but all Duke had to do was walk in the room with that nice suit on, smile his dazzling smile and flash those big brown eyes of his, and everyone reconsidered their boycott. Macy found it best to hold her grudge against him. To have a crush on him from afar was one thing; it was a different story when he was in the flesh, flirting with her. And it was obvious yesterday evening that he had been hitting on her.

Macy had caught Duke staring at her quite a bit at the party but refused to give him eye contact. A man like him probably had a hundred women throwing themselves at him. And then there was the horrible way he got himself introduced. He should have been ashamed of himself for putting Pablo and Monique in a position like that. But that didn't stop him. He actually had the nerve to try to hire her. She was glad she had a busy schedule. She had five homes to decorate tomorrow, and then every day until a week before Christmas she was busy.

The heavy bells on top of the door chimed. Macy perked up. Despite her dislike for Duke's personality, Macy felt her heart sink a tad when she spied her assistant Serena Berks coming in the door. She had no idea why she would even think a man like Duke Rodriguez would come to her place of business. She didn't know what she would have done with him if he had shown up, but then a devilish little voice nagged at the back of her mind, reminding her that it hadn't been *that* long since she knew what to do with a man.

Down the hall, there came a grunting, a cursing and a sniffling. Poor Serena was dragging in a huge plastic mouse statue with all her might. At five foot two, Serena was just two inches shorter than Macy. The giant mouse, decked out in a red-and-green stitched scarf, had to have been about five seven. Serena's bobbed red hair was disheveled around her freckled face.

Macy had hoped to find one or both of the male assistants she'd hired to help lift and cart around some of the heavier decorations. It was the peak season for exterior holiday decorating and the musclemen, Spencer and Andy, hadn't shown up. Usually, they broke the frat boy stereotype by being reliable. But late last night Spencer had left an apologetic message about not being here this week. She prayed it was a horrible prank.

Getting up from her desk, Macy peered down the hall to where she had a view of the front door. She shook her head and hid her smile as she twisted her hair into a bun and secured it with her pencil.

"Hey," Macy pouted. "Santa didn't announce your presence."

"That's because I threatened him within an inch of his life if he called me a *ho* one more time." Serena projected her voice a little louder so that it could be heard upstairs and in the backyard. "A lil' help here!"

"We're the only ones here," Macy shouted as she walked back to her desk and closed her sketchbook.

The outline of the Wainwrights' lawn was just about done. She hoped they would be happy with it. They'd better be happy. This would be the third time changing things around, and Macy's time was precious, not to mention that her staff seemed to be dwindling for the Thanksgiving holiday.

"Here," Macy offered, picking up the pace down the steps and into the foyer, "let me help."

"No, you don't have to," Serena argued as she stood the mouse in his upright position. The unplugged giant mouse stood with a black nose, which, when plugged in, turned red. The plastic book of Christmas carols in his hand was open. From a distance no one could read the words, but up close someone had written, "Who let the dogs out?" as a silly joke.

"Where are the boys?"

Biting her bottom lip, Macy hesitated to tell Serena the truth. From the looks of her dust-covered garnet-and-gold T-shirt and jean shorts, the bookkeeper's morning had started off rough. She must have climbed over everything in the shed just to find the mouse. Going into the storage space went above and beyond the call of duty.

At thirty, Serena had been her assistant for the last four years while she worked on her BS and now her MBA at Florida State University. She was a pencil pusher who kept up with Macy's schedules and appointments, yet here she was doing all the grunt work. She wondered if Serena would believe that the boys had been toppled over by a giant snowball. It was highly unlikely. The weather for Thanksgiving was scheduled to be a balmy seventy-eight degrees.

"They left an apologetic message on my answering machine saying they left early for Thanksgiving. I kind of hoped they were joking."

"No way! I thought they agreed to be here over the break."

Macy rested her hands on her hips as she studied the mouse. "I know. But according to the message, they somehow—" she rested her finger on her chin to recall the exact way the boys had phrased it "—scored some serious tickets." She mocked Spencer's surfer-boy accent with air quotes.

Serena's laugh turned into a hacking cough. She shook her strawberry-tinted head. "That's pretty lame of them. They worked last year. They understand how this is the busiest weekend for you."

Shrugging, Macy tried to smile, already figuring how to handle things. In a way, she looked forward to working alone tomorrow and Friday. She was prepared.

Key organizational skills helped keep Macy sane. What took most grown men all day to do, she could complete in an hour. She had a few homes in the morning with light decorations. Extra hands stringing up the lights might have been nice, but Macy could handle the work; after all, she'd started this business ten years ago with no help.

The only stickler in her plans was the Wainwrights' home, simply because they kept changing their ideas. Typically the slots for holiday decorations got booked up by the Fourth of July. Every weekend until just before Christmas, she was busy. Most trusted Macy's ideas. A lot of homeowners' associations even required their neighborhoods to decorate unless religion prohibited it. Doing the work on her own wasn't a problem, especially since the kids were at her former in-laws' house. Perhaps it would be a bit of a hassle trying to unload her truck, but she could get it done.

"Achoo." Serena sneezed.

Panic ripped through Macy's body. With the boys gone, she was going to have to lean on Serena more. "Are you okay?" she asked slowly.

"Just a sneeze," Serena said, swatting the mouse on the ear. "He did this to me, stupid dusty thing...*achoo*!"

Macy raised her left eyebrow in question. "Maybe you ought to drink some orange juice just in case. C'mon, I believe I spotted some when I put up some leftovers last night."

"Maybe," Serena answered as she followed Macy. "Oh, and I forgot to tell you who I ran into yesterday while you went to the party. Remember the party I wasn't invited to?"

"Who?" Macy asked with a sigh, anticipating Serena's guilt trip.

The sound of their footsteps on the hardwood floors blocked out Serena's exasperated sigh as they crossed the former living room, now a sitting room. Macy straightened a Christmas ornament on a seven-foot Fraser fir tree and kicked one of the shiny green display presents with red polka dots out of the walkway. On the other side of the stairs, across from the living room, was once Macy's dining room, now two downstairs offices. In the back of the house was the kitchen; access was gained from the thin hallway from the offices or directly straight back from the front door and living room. Macy opened the white double-door refrigerator. Pictures of previous jobs she'd had over the years mingled with Gia's and MJ's old drawings.

"I saw Mr. Officer and a Gentleman."

"Who?"

"Ugh, Lawrence, the pilot you dated."

Macy hardly called going out with Lawrence Hobbs dating. The whole reason Macy had gutted her Victorian home was to meet clients here in the spacious waiting room or in one of the back offices, or even better, at their homes to better survey the landscape. Lawrence, on the other hand, had one reason or another to meet her at a coffee shop, café and even the park to pick her brain about decorating. Eventually, the two of them figured out that Serena should do all the scheduling. Lawrence, a sweet man, had retired from the air force

and settled down in Tallahassee. At the party yesterday, someone mentioned he'd started his own private
airline, albeit a small one.

"You mean the pilot you kept leaving me alone with
when he came over here?"

"Yes. I think he seemed really interested in how
you were doing. I think you ought to give him another
chance."

"Really?" Macy said very quizzically with a raised
eyebrow. "Because when I saw him yesterday as well, at
said party you weren't invited to, Lawrence mentioned
his new girlfriend, one of the judges from last year's
holiday decoration contest."

Serena opened her mouth, but closed it quickly. Her
matchmaking skills were lost on this case, no matter
how hard she tried. This time of year, dating was out of
the question for Macy. Macy smiled and thought of her
children and how they would react if she started dating. Their father, Mario, dated. Hell, he'd been dating
before they divorced.

Macy shook her head as she bent over to look for
something nutritious for Serena. These days, Macy kept
the refrigerator stocked with various juices from orange to grape and apple. Today, she seemed to have
only orange left. Next to the drinks were containers of
leftover turkey and all the fixings. She'd made extra
plates last night for herself and the boys to eat after
work. Now realizing they weren't coming in, she had
extra extra leftovers. Grabbing a glass from the dish-
washer, Macy poured Serena some juice and patted the
bar stool. "Drink up."

"Orange?" She frowned, being ornery. "But I don't like orange."

"Beggars can't be choosers, Serena."

"But I'm not begging." Serena tried to argue, but Macy just stared at her. Playfully pouting, Serena climbed onto the high-backed bar stool. "Fine, I'll drink even though I'm not sick. So what do you think about Lawrence?"

"I don't think much about him," Macy answered honestly. Lawrence was a nice-looking man. He was about five eleven with cocoa-brown skin and a trimmed beard; his was one of many faces Macy had seen yesterday. He had come over and given her a hug and thanked her again for the work she'd done on his house, but told her this year there were so many changes in his life that he wouldn't be around to enjoy the decorations.

Serena rolled her eyes and gave a huff. "He was looking mighty hot when I saw him. He was on his way to the party I wasn't invited to."

But was he as hot as Duke Rodriguez? a little voice nagged in the back of Macy's brain.

"Hmph." Serena's eyebrows rose. "That was a pretty funny look you just gave. Did you meet someone? Oh, wait, tell me—how was meeting Mr. Dimples?"

With a droll eye roll, Macy shook her head at the nickname her thirteen-year-old daughter had given the obnoxious anchorman. Serena didn't help matters whenever Gia came to the office after school. They had been fans of the anchorman before he came to Tallahassee, and now they were bursting at the seams at him being here. Gia had actually wanted to miss going to her grandparents' house for the week just so she could go to the Baezes' holiday party and see Duke.

"Exactly as I expected."

That had been the understatement of the year. He was also a bit more than what she'd expected. Monique warned her ahead of time that Pablo had invited Duke home for some old-fashioned Dominican cuisine. He'd arrived in a bright red Ferrari, and parked front and center of the driveway for everyone to see as they entered the house. She'd spied him the minute he walked in. Duke was good-looking, but of course he knew that. He was the only one in the room wearing a two-thousand-dollar suit. The average household in Tallahassee brought that in during one month.

"Oh my God, did you speak to him?"

"He spoke." Macy shrugged.

"Were you nice to him?"

"I spoke," Macy said with a coy smile.

The last thing Macy had said to Serena about Duke before the party was that she was going to give him a piece of her mind when she saw him. She'd come into the office seething on the morning of the incident, demanding to know where he got off telling the world that there was no Santa Claus. Andy and Spencer had sworn they'd never seen Macy so worked up before. Velda Thompson, her grandmother, had taught her to always act rationally. It was a long and hard lesson for Macy to learn, but she thought this situation deserved a few foul words. Grandma V must have been rolling around in her grave.

"Did you give him a piece of your mind?"

"I told that athle-tante…"

"Oh-em-gee!" Serena stopped her with squealing. She sounded just like Gia. "Please tell me you did not call him that."

Macy shrugged. "I may have."

"I'm going to die of embarrassment. He probably thinks you're some sort of freak."

She couldn't have been that much of a freak if the man still tried to come on to her. Macy decided to omit the part about Duke's nerve to hit on her at the party. Serena was always trying to push single men in her direction, despite Macy's lack of time for one. Her business was booming, and when she wasn't working, her kids kept her busy. But that never stopped her assistant from trying. Serena would always bail her out of meetings after she did a background check on the single men. She claimed that seven years of not dating, let alone no sex, was not good for a woman.

But Macy had brushed off Duke's flirting as she did with most of the men she'd come across. A lot of men tried to use the excuse of hiring her for a job. Duke Rodriguez was no different than the rest. Well, he might have been hotter than any man she'd ever laid eyes on, but what did it matter? She had no time for someone like him. And he had no time for her. Duke wasn't going to be in town long, and Macy saw no reason to start something that couldn't be finished. Monique was only on maternity leave until after the Christmas holidays. She would return with the coverage of ringing in the New Year. Her stance on dating, even if it was Duke Rodriguez, wasn't going to change. So what if he had those deep dimples or those luscious lips that made even eating food look sexy?

"Answer my question." Serena took a long sip of juice, but kept her eyes on her boss. "What happened?"

"Nothing happened, per se. He did ask if I could work for him."

The news made Serena choke. Macy didn't believe her for one minute. She was the mother of two kids who always tried faking sick. Finally Serena settled down and asked, "And you turned him down?"

"As it is, we're already short-staffed, and you're getting sick. How am I going to take on another client?"

"I'm not sick," Serena said, fighting back a sneeze. Macy watched Serena's eyes redden as she tried to hold it in. If she wasn't getting sick, then she was having a major allergic reaction to something. Her nose was a faint pink.

Macy folded her arms across her chest and leaned against the counter. "Want to bet?"

"I am working through this. I need to hear good things. Tell me more about him, Macy," she whined.

"What is there to tell?" Macy's upper lip curled. "He is a typical man."

"Ugh! You are so lucky you met him," Serena moaned. "I wish I could have."

The doors over the glass front door opened with a jingle. The Santa monitor went off with a deep *ho ho ho*. Serena made a funny face the minute Macy got up to walk over to the door. Serena had closed her eyes, crossed her fingers and begun chanting.

"*I wish I could win a million dollars. I wish I could win a million dollars.*"

The wonders of that girl never ceased to entertain Macy. Serena was always doing something superstitious like that. She thought if she spoke a person's name out loud and the person appeared, the same thing might happen if she spoke out loud her next wish, usually concerning money. Every time she drove by a graveyard she held her breath and crossed herself; she picked up pennies on their tails off the ground and turned them over so the next person could have good luck. Macy headed out the kitchen doorway to catch a glimpse of her customer. Instantly, her throat went dry and she felt that whiplash appeal in her neck at the sight.

There, standing by her sexy Santa, stood the one and only Duke Rodriguez, dressed down compared to yesterday. Gone was the custom-made suit, but what he had on was still just as bad: jeans made to fit his long, powerful legs, a blue T-shirt that fit across his broad chest just a little too tight and a black leather coat that probably cost the same as her fee for one Christmas-decorated house. His dark hair was cropped against his head, framing his olive-skinned face. And as he smiled, knowing she was ogling him, his deep dimples popping out as he had the nerve to modestly blush. He could have easily stepped out of the pages of *GQ* magazine.

She knew she'd been clear yesterday when she said she was too busy. "Can I help you?"

"I certainly hope so," Duke said with a dangerous, juicy, bad-boy grin. He caught Serena's attention and nodded his dark head in her direction. "Hey, how are you? I'm Duke..."

"Rodriguez," Serena answered for him as she moved with lightning-like speed, nearly bowling Macy over just to shake his hand. "I know. Second-string shortstop for the Yankees for two seasons before you started work as a sports correspondent, prime-time anchor on ESPN for a few years, and then working from New York and DC. I've followed your career. We're so glad to have you in our little small town."

"Well, who knew a high school kid like yourself would be so into the news? I'm flattered."

The person most flattered was Serena. She gave an unrecognizable high-pitched giggle and swayed back and forth. Her face was the same color as the red in her shirt. Macy refrained from rolling her eyes as Serena beamed at his flattery. "Oh, no, I'm not in high school."

"This is my assistant, Serena." Macy made the quick introduction to keep Serena from making a bigger fool of herself. "What do you want, Mr. Rodriguez?"

"Now, didn't I tell you that my friends call me Duke?"

Macy raised an eyebrow and folded her arms across the front of her short-sleeved red sweater. "Mr. Rodriguez."

Serena gently reached over to wrap her arm around Macy's shoulder. She squeezed her just a little too hard. "Excuse my boss. She's a bit delusional."

Duke nodded and smiled. "I see. Well, I was hoping that was the case yesterday when I asked for Macy's services."

"I told you yesterday, Mr. Rodriguez."

"Duke," he corrected.

It was useless. She could spend the rest of the afternoon playing this Abbott and Costello bit over whether or not to call him Duke or Mr. Rodriguez. Macy huffed and caved in. The sooner he left, the sooner she could get back to work. "Fine. I told you the situation yesterday, *Duke*. I simply don't have time to decorate your house."

"I'll pay double."

"No."

"Please hear me out." Duke held his large hands out, pleading. Macy spied how smooth they were, compared to hers. Subconsciously she wrung her calloused hands together. A celebrity athlete like him was used to snapping his fingers and having people, specifically women, jump to his aid. Well, Macy knew she wasn't one of those women. If he wanted her help, he should have booked her six months to a year in advance, like the rest of her clients. "I'm begging. I came home yesterday and someone had egged my front porch."

"Damn kids." Serena *tsk*ed and shook her head.

"The sad thing is that I don't think it's the kids. It's the mothers in my neighborhood. The day before that, someone hung Santa in a tree and toilet-papered my house. I spent all night trying to get 'Santa Killer' off my front door."

An image of Duke standing in his doorway in nothing but a pair of red basketball shorts while scrubbing the door with a sponge and a foamy white bucket of soap entered her mind. She could picture the muscles on his back flexing as he held on to the door for balance while he reached down and soaked his sponge. A warm glow spread up Macy's chest as she blinked the image out of her mind and focused her gaze on her guest. "I'm really sorry for what you're going through, but I'm sure things will blow over."

"You know, I could always come over and stake out your place for you," Serena chimed in.

A tint of red touched Duke's cheeks. "Thanks, but I think what I really need to do is throw a good old-fashioned Christmas party just to show everyone that I'm not the ogre that they seem to think. Outing Santa was an accident."

"Sure, just like telling that athlete he needed a vasectomy, or telling a teen actress that she might want to consider dropping her parents as managers," Macy ticked off. "Or what about you telling that singer that he ought to come out of the closet?"

"So you've followed my work?" He wiggled his eyebrows at her. His mouth opened wide into a smile. She hated that she thought about how kissable his lips looked right now.

Perhaps wiggling his eyebrows was a dealmaker when getting a woman to come home with him, but Macy reminded herself that she wasn't interested. To prove it, Macy rolled her eyes and feigned disinterest with a slight yawn. "My thirteen-year-old daughter follows you. I just happen to be the type of parent that monitors what she watches."

"And so she and your eight-year-old son were watching?" He cocked his head to the side and grinned. "And you were watching me, too?"

Shifting her weight from one heel to the other, Macy shrugged her shoulders. "For your information, I happen to watch the show every morning. I was doing that before Monique went on maternity leave." The slow, lopsided smile Duke gave her was admittedly sexy. His attempt at what he must have considered his A-game was sad. "But I may start watching the other channel."

"See, that's exactly what I'm trying to avoid."

"Perhaps we need to sit down for this," Serena said.

Looking over at her, Macy noticed that her assistant was breaking out in a sweat. The last thing she wanted was for Serena to get sick. She had finals coming up soon and she needed all the studying she could get. This was exactly why she wanted the boys here this weekend: because she wanted to give Serena a break.

"Yes, please come in and have a seat." She stepped aside and waved her hand to the left, toward the parlor area. The hardwood floors echoed with the heavy footsteps of his rather large feet. Duke sat down in the Queen Anne chair and crossed one leg over the other. He filled the chair like royalty. Serena sat beside him on the adjacent matching couch, still batting her eyes at him. Macy stepped into the kitchen first to grab Serena's glass of juice.

Once everyone was situated, Macy sat down and sighed. "So what is it you're trying to avoid?"

"Well." Duke placed both feet on the ground, rested his elbows on his thighs and leaned forward. "You seem to care about Monique, and you are aware Pablo is practically my brother. I just want to do a good job for them.

I would hate for Monique lose her viewers due to my stupidity."

"Aw, you are so sweet," Serena cooed, leaning forward in her seat. She folded her hands underneath her chin and cocked her head to the side. It looked uncomfortable as she sipped on her juice.

If the girl flirted any more, she'd be sitting in his lap. Macy shook her head at her. Was she really going to believe this? It was a ploy, Macy thought. Somehow, Serena was doing one of her matchmaking schemes. Macy leaned back in the chair opposite him and studied his face.

"I told you, I don't have time. On top of everything else, two of my employees took off this weekend, which is going to push any time that I have to the limit."

"What if I paid triple?"

With that, Serena choked on her juice again.

Macy ignored her. "It doesn't work like that, Duke. I have limited time."

"Well, technically, you just have the homes tomorrow to do for the ones that are out of town." Serena offered up the schedule. "Too bad we're missing our handymen to help out." She gave Duke a wink. Reaching out, Serena touched Duke's biceps. "Oh my, what big muscles you have."

He at least had the sense to blush. "Thank you."

"Serena." Macy sent a warning glance at her friend. "Control yourself."

"What? I'm just pointing out that our usual muscle guys are going to the big game this weekend and I guess they drove down early."

"So I can help," Duke said excitedly. "I'm off until Monday, but even still, after that I am done with the morning news by seven. I can help you during the day with your work, and that will free up your time to help me throw my party, right?"

Serena sat back in the couch and grinned, ignoring the evil glare Macy shot her. "Beggars can't be choosers, Macy. Besides, don't forget that the boys are going to have exams coming up soon, so they're not going to be able to help out as much over the next few weeks."

"No." Macy shook her head.

"Why not?" Duke asked.

Serena leaned forward and faced Macy, putting her hand over the side of her face so that Duke couldn't see what she was saying, even though her whisper didn't do what it was supposed to. "He's paying triple, Macy. With your new house, the additional sheds you've ordered and the two trucks, the money will come in handy. Remember, I do the books…it'd be nice to see a chunk in there."

"No," Macy hissed.

"Why not?" Duke and Serena chorused.

"For starters, we typically meet up at four in the morning."

"Um." Duke cleared his throat. "I'm doing the morning news. I'm always up at four."

There was nothing more Macy wanted to do than to protest, but if she did she would only look silly. Monique and Pablo were her dear friends. They were the first people to help her get her business started, by offering free advertising. Every year, she decorated their home for free, just because she felt she owed them. What Duke had done was stupid, but Macy also knew he could be the cause of viewers leaving Monique's show. She couldn't let that happen.

She could handle working with Duke. She could handle his cockiness. Lord knew she'd been through worse with Mario. Macy gave Duke a once-over. She still doubted, regardless of his solid six-foot-four frame, that he had ever done manual labor. Had he been on a ladder? Could he string lights? Would he know how to test if one bulb was broken and what to do if it was?

Macy's mental argument raged on in her head. He'd be more in the way than anything else. And more likely Duke would ask to work inside. If that were the case, she figured he'd sit inside half the time while she stayed outdoors. That would work out perfectly, because then she wouldn't have to spend too much time with him.

Folding her arms across her chest, she looked at him and reluctantly said, "Fine."

"Well, that settles that," Duke beamed. "I'm all yours."

Chapter 3

The pot of coffee finished percolating at the same time someone knocked softly on the door. Macy stopped briefly on the bottom step in the waiting room and glanced at the grandfather clock chiming away at four in the morning. Since the kids were spending Thanksgiving with their father and his family this holiday season, she'd stayed at work last night. She slept in her old bedroom, curled up with anticipation for her day with Duke Rodriguez. Fortunately, Serena was going to act as a buffer.

Macy had awoken thirty minutes ago. *And what a wasted thirty minutes it was.* Not only had the Wainwrights rejected her latest designs she had bike-messengered over last night, she'd spent the first minutes trying to figure out if each pair of jeans she had in the closet of her bedroom made her look too bulky. When did she ever worry about her clothes? First thing in the morning and Duke already flustered her. Ten minutes ago, she'd settled on a pair of dark-washed jeans, comfy gray furry boots and an over-size long-sleeve gray shirt.

Cutting into the silence of the early-morning hours of the house was another knock. Macy literally stood still until the third knock, still debating whether or not she would greet Duke at the door before or after her first sip of coffee, or even let him in. She decided on the latter and opened the door. Sexy Santa greeted her with his usual *ho-ho-ho* greeting, which made her grin as she did so.

"Good morning," she said sweetly. Her fingers twisted the scrunchie wrapped around the doorknob and maneuvered the band to her wrist.

Duke Rodriguez filled the doorway with the essence of a man. Macy braced herself against the door's frame to stabilize herself from her weakening knees. He wore another pair of well-fitting jeans that hung low enough on his hips, a black V-neck T-shirt and a pair of classic wheat Timberland boots. The front part of his shirt was tucked into his jeans, showing off the obvious silhouette of his washboard abs. His face had a slight morning stubble, which made him look even more rugged. His mouth opened wide as he smiled at her. "And good morning to you!" he said cheerfully.

"I didn't think you'd really come." Macy held the door wider. "Come on in, the coffee just finished brewing." She braced her back against the door, watching him stroll inside, and then pressed the door closed with the weight of her body. "You drink coffee, don't you?" she asked, walking past him. While she twisted and secured her hair into a high ponytail with the tie around her wrist, she listened for his heavy footsteps following her into the kitchen.

"I'm Dominican," Duke said with a heavily accented, matter-of-fact yet pompous tone.

He was Dominican? As if that was an answer! Of course she knew of his Dominican heritage. Duke put the "Spang" in Spanglish, flipping from English to Spanish at the drop of a hat depending on the person he was interviewing, typically making grown women swoon. Macy groaned inwardly when she realized that it seemed as if she knew everything about him.

He was Pablo's best friend.

He was Gia's major crush.

Macy knew just about everything there was to know about the man, whether she wanted to or not. She knew he was born and raised in Mao, a city in the province of Valverde, played baseball well enough to earn him a scholarship to the States, played with the Yankees for a while and then used his major in broadcast journalism to become a sportscaster, landing him his major break as a serious journalist during the 9/11 attacks. Duke's voice had brought her out of a dark time in her life.

The 2001 attacks had sent Macy into a depression. Having lost her journalist parents, who died in a car accident heading to cover the aftermath of the World Trade Center bombing, Macy stayed up night and day watching the coverage. Had her parents been alive, they'd no doubt have injected themselves into the report as well, the thought of which, crazy as it was, infuriated Macy once again. Their desire to cover the news had always overshadowed staying at home and raising their little girl. But there was something about the way Duke reported the news, the way he let his genuine emotions out, that struck a chord with her. Without having old video of her parents reporting, Macy had never felt the bond. Duke stood in front of the rubble and as he helped the people surrounding him, he helped her see the human side of a reporter and somehow forgive her parents. Sometimes she felt she owed Duke everything.

The infatuation had died when he outed Santa.

"We can grab a cup before we go out. Maybe Serena will call by then."

Instead of sitting at the kitchen bar, waiting to be served, Duke stepped into the kitchen and lifted the carafe. The black liquid brew steamed from the top. Through the short sleeve of his T-shirt, the bulge of muscle of his biceps caught Macy's eye. Obviously the man worked out. She never noticed how small the eight-cup maker looked until it was in his hands.

"Where do you keep your cups?" Duke asked.

"Up there." Macy nodded toward the closed cabinet above the sink and headed to the refrigerator. "So because you're Dominican, it's automatic that you like coffee? My dad was half Italian. Should I automatically like pasta?"

"Well, of course, and if you're making *baccalà* for the Feast of the Seven Fishes on Christmas Eve, count me in!" Duke half smiled over his shoulder.

She was shocked he knew of those traditions. When

most families had a nice turkey or ham or even a pizza on Christmas Eve, Macy grew up eating various seafood dishes, from *baccalà*, or salted cod, all the way to lobster ravioli. Christmas Eve was a day when most Italians fasted until Midnight Mass. "It has yet to be determined if you are invited or not."

"Well, I have a few weeks to win you over."

She turned so he could see her roll her eyes. He just grinned even wider. "Anyway, you like coffee?"

"I just simply meant that I grew up in the Dominican Republic, where generations and generations of my family worked on coffee plantations. Besides milk, it was probably the one thing I drank all the time."

"Well, there goes that myth," Macy mumbled, casting a glance up and down his frame.

"What myth?"

She hadn't realized he'd heard her. "I'm always telling my son that drinking coffee will stunt his growth."

The left eyebrow on his handsome face lifted in a question. "Your son, the eight-year-old, drinks coffee?"

"He wants to do what his mom and dad do," Macy explained, shaking the two cream bottles from the fridge as she chose her words wisely. Typically most men toned down the flirting mode when she mentioned a father in the picture.

"Oh?"

Did she hear a fleck of disappointment in his voice as he set the cups down on the counter? Glancing over to see if he was looking at her, which he wasn't, she noticed his biceps again as he reached for the cups in front of him.

The infatuation she swore had died out now reignited. Her knees weakened, and she reached for the counter behind her. *Muscles shouldn't make me weak.* Mario had muscles for days and she never got so gaga over them. *Focus*, she told herself. She watched his long fingers wrap around a mug. She liked that he chose a Santa cup and a snowman cup. There were plain old-fashioned ones up there, but given that her place of business centered around Christmas, she liked to keep the theme going for clients.

"So, where's your husband when you're out working?" Duke asked with his back turned. His voice had changed from disappointed to nonchalant. Perhaps he was trying to cover for hitting on a married woman. A slight tinge of guilt hit her. She turned, ready to face him, when he turned around. He had such broad shoulders that fell down into a tapered waist. It was a shame he was sculptured so beautifully.

"He's home with his parents and the kids." She shut the door with her hip and brought the creamers toward him. "I have Christmas Ginger and Holiday Hazelnut. And I don't have a husband."

"But you said…" Duke came back to the other side of the kitchen; he leaned a hip against the counter and placed his elbow on top of it to lower himself to her height. She noticed that all morning long, while she'd been sketching hard jawlines, she hadn't realized that Duke's cheeks slightly resembled a chipmunk's, which made him look very boyish. He nodded his head. "You said 'mom and dad.'"

Macy raised her eyebrow and matched his smile. "Well, in your defense, I did. So what do you want?"

He blinked during the long pause while their eyes locked. Macy's breathing became shallow, and she prayed he did not notice. Finally he shook his head. "Oh, you mean the cream?"

What else could she have meant? When his left eyebrow rose devilishly, Macy quickly got the point of her open question. A once-forgotten pitter-patter fluttered in the pit of her stomach. "Yes, the cream."

"I'll take mine black."

Macy shrugged and poured some of the hazelnut in her Santa cup. "I have this sinking feeling that Serena isn't coming today," she confessed out of nowhere. Maybe she just wanted to let him know up front that it was going to be a long day with just the two of them. She wasn't sure if she could trust herself to be around him all day long. "You're more than welcome to back out if you want."

Without even blowing, Duke lifted the snowman to his mouth and drank. "I'm staying."

"It's Thanksgiving, you know."

"And happy Thanksgiving to you." Duke grinned, tilting his cup in cheer. "Stop trying to come up with excuses. You can't do all this yourself." He waved one hand in the air at the decorations.

"You don't even know what *this*—" she mocked his movement with her free hand over her head "—is."

"Technically, you *can* hang up Christmas decorations all by yourself." Duke set his drink down. "You did do it all yourself before, didn't you? Climb trees and string lights, haul all your own stuff that you have stored in a warehouse not far from here. But just because you can doesn't mean I'm going to let you. Speaking of which, there wasn't a car in sight on my way over here, so we should make good time to get back here at nine so you can watch the parade."

Truly flattered, Macy beamed and bit back a smile. "I see you did your research and watched the video on me?"

When Macy first got up and running, Monique had done a piece on Winter Paradise, Macy's decorating business. She and her cameraman followed Macy around when she didn't have any help. It was just the promotion she needed. The video was now ten years old. The segment had ended with Macy climbing onto her couch in her red-and-white-striped footy pajamas, cuddling next to a then-three-year-old Gia. Although Macy wished that part could have been on the editing floor. She'd decorated Monique's house for free as long as Mo promised never to show the clip again. Duke had to have gone to great lengths to find it in the old tapes at the studio.

"I like to know what and who I'm working with." He nodded and slowly smiled. "So I went home last night, studied you. You're very impressive."

Heat from her blush toasted her cheeks. Duke Rodriguez stood in her kitchen, giving her compliments. Slowly Macy tried to relax, resting her hip against the counter. "Not everyone enjoys Christmas as much as I do. I might be the only person who gets goose bumps when stores start putting out holiday decorations before Halloween."

"I don't know about Halloween." Duke winked. "Someday I'll have to tell you how we celebrate Christmas in my hometown."

"It doesn't even snow there," Macy teased easily.

"And seventy degrees is ideal Christmas weather?"

Macy raised her eyebrow. Touché. "Well, the weather will be colder come Christmas."

He nodded his head in honorable acceptance of her comment. "I have to say, I watched your video over and over." He glanced around the kitchen, letting out a long sigh. "So this is where you raised your kids?"

"Yep, up until this year."

"I bet you have a big tree."

She nodded, admitting the truth. "What about you? Are you going to put up a tree?"

"Sure, if you think I need one."

For a moment, she forgot that she was going to decorate his place. "Oh yeah, right."

"Did you forget about me just that fast?" he teased.

As if, taunted a voice in the back of her mind.

"I bet with your reputation around town, you're able to get the best tree."

"The first tree," Macy boasted, "although this year, I don't have time to get the first one."

He smiled back at her. "I bet you're like royalty around here."

"Nah, I just like to make sure that everyone is happy through the holidays."

Nodding, Duke leaned against the counter, mirroring her. Through half-closed lids, his eyes focused on her lips. Self-consciously, Macy licked them, wondering freakishly what it would be like if he kissed her right now. Her throat went dry, and she couldn't think of a thing to say. The silence growing between them only provided more time for her to stare at him with her naughty thoughts. She prayed for a break in the awkward quietness. She prayed for anything to stop the wanton thoughts she was having about this man she barely knew. *C'mon, Serena, show up!*

Finally he spoke. "So how did you get the name Macy?"

"Well." Macy took a sip of coffee first, glad for the distraction from watching him staring at her mouth. She had thought for a moment that he was going to kiss her. And if he had, she might not have moved. "I was born during the Macy's Thanksgiving Day parade."

If he hadn't choked on his coffee, the surprised news would certainly have shown on his face. Duke's eyes opened wide; his mouth hung agape. "What?"

She gave him a slow smile. "It's true. My mother was a local weather girl who insisted on covering the parade. My father was also an anchorman. They lived in Jersey and commuted to New York City. Since my mom wasn't due until New Year's Eve, she thought everything would be okay. Then, just as Snoopy was coming down Thirty-Fourth Street, her water broke, contractions came and they hid her in a float."

"You're joking."

"Nope." She took another sip and hid her smile behind her mug. "Somewhere in this universe is a recording of my public entrance into the world."

"Interesting." Duke's melodic hum sent a wave of chills down her spine. "How did you end up in Tallahassee?"

With a shrug, Macy sighed. "Well, with my parents busy covering the world news, my grandparents took me in."

Duke straightened to his six-foot-plus frame and raked his hand over his cropped black hair. "That's pretty cool. My family believes in closeness. Hey, wait a minute, today must be your birthday, right?"

"No, this year my birthday falls on a Sunday."

He pressed his lips together as if to make a mental note about it. *He didn't have to*, she thought to herself. They just met two days ago.

Technically.

Surely, with all the chatter between the two of them, she felt they knew each other already. She knew all about Duke's career choices, and she knew all about his relationships with the starlets he'd interviewed over the years. She also knew about the serious relationship he had been in. If Gia hadn't mentioned it, Serena would have, or Macy could have easily caught wind of it in the grocery store line, looking at the tabloids.

Up until recently, Duke Rodriguez had been with a tall, raven-haired beauty named Kristina Barclay. They'd been together for about a year, which at least told Macy that the man was able to commit to a relationship. And then over the summer, they'd split, and neither would comment as to why.

Soon after their separation, Duke had been photographed at every nightclub from DC to New York City with one gorgeous leggy woman or another. Macy just assumed it was because Duke probably didn't want to settle down. He was close to forty and set in his own ways. Why else would a grown man leave a perfectly good job at a national news station in DC and travel down south just to help out a friend?

"Big plans? It's your what? Twenty-eighth?"

"Nice try." She smirked. "But if you didn't figure out from the interview, then I'm not going to tell."

She watched him stretch. She'd never paid attention to a man stretch before. It never seemed erotic, yet he managed to make it so. Heat crept around her neck, down her chest. Duke's chest seemed to double in size as he inhaled. His stretch came with a groan, a low, grunted sound that rose from the pit of his belly to his Adam's apple. When he finished with his yawn and stretch, he leaned against the counter, both elbows on the countertop. He seemed closer to her. And with him bent over like that, he was eye level with her.

"I am sure I can figure it out." He was confident in what he said and the way he smiled at her. She wished he'd stop doing that, because every time he did, she felt like a schoolgirl with a crazy crush. "So let me get this straight. Both your parents were in broadcasting and you're giving me grief about my slipup? Are you saying every broadcast was perfect?"

"Of course they did slip up every now and then. But it's just different when it's your own kids."

"I guess I would understand more if I had kids of my own."

"None?"

He shook his head no and reached for his coffee again. "No."

"Too busy planning your own career?" Macy said with a snarky smirk.

"Actually, I found out when I entered college at Miami."

Macy recalled her grandfather boasting about Duke's reputation as a third baseman phenom. The major leagues were interested in recruiting him. Even at eighteen, tall and lanky, his dark Caribbean looks had caused a buzz. Now here he stood in the flesh, filled out in all the right places, and still causing quite the buzz. Macy swallowed hard and pushed down the memory of all the fantasies she had of him.

"I came to the States for a summer workshop and got pretty sick. The docs worried it was meningitis, but turned out I had mumps again."

"Mumps?" Macy repeated, cocking her head to the side. She tried to imagine Duke's square jawline swollen.

"Turns out I am one of the few people who can contract it a second time," he continued, "especially since I was never vaccinated as a child."

"Second?" Macy shook her head. "I don't understand."

"I told you my folks worked on a coffee plantation. They really couldn't afford to take the day off to take me to the doctor. "

It was her turn for her mouth to drop wide open. "Seriously? What kind of damages can that cause?"

"You mean, besides not being able to have kids?"

Macy's mouth opened with shock. For every interview Duke did on television, someone had always turned the question around on him and asked about his desire to settle down with a wife and children. Now perhaps she understood about not having any children. "I'm so sorry," she breathed.

Duke chuckled nervously. "I don't know why I just told you about that." He pressed his lips together, flattening them against his teeth. "Yep, but don't feel bad for me. I have the Baez kids that love me, and I love them as if they were my own. I get to spoil them without having to do any of the potty training."

"Ha! I'd love to see you changing diapers."

"Hey, I've changed my share. I just never want to go through getting a kid up every single night to go to the bathroom." He let out a visible shiver as if the reminder brought back bad memories. Macy had to laugh. She had had her share of sleepless nights with MJ and Gia.

"You're sweet to help them out." Maybe he wasn't such a prima donna.

"They're the sweet ones for sharing their kids with me, considering my situation." Duke blinked; his long lashes only made her envious. "So far, the kids still look at me as their hero when Mami and Papi won't buy them what they want."

With a combination of a groan and a laugh, Macy shook her head. "You and Serena would make a perfect couple, ya know." She cleared her throat and rubbed the back of her neck at how uncomfortable the words sounded out loud. Duke was not hers to even claim for herself or anyone else, but the thought of seeing him intimate with someone didn't sit well with her. He was still inches away from her face.

Duke glanced at the counter where she nervously fiddled with her cup of coffee. He reached down with his forefinger and stroked the side of her finger. As expected, his hands were soft and warm. An unexpected result was the flight of the butterflies in her belly. He leaned closer. Macy watched him tilt his head as he approached. Her breath was caught in her throat.

"Thanks for the offer, but—" he brushed his lips gently across hers "—I feel it's important you know that I am extremely interested in you."

"Extremely?" Macy squeaked out. Her heart thudded against her rib cage so loudly that she just knew he could hear it.

"Extremely and only."

To confirm his words, Duke pressed his lips against her. He tasted like coffee, strong and sweet. His mouth moved with an expertise that she'd never experienced before. Their connection was magnetic. His bottom lip curved perfectly against hers. Regardless of their height difference, their bodies fit together like a glove, molding against each other. His large hands supported her lower back, pulling her close to him. She could feel the hardness of his body, and swayed. Macy closed her eyes and allowed the feeling to take over her body. It was as though she was floating on a cloud and she never wanted to come down. She could be kissed like this forever. But forever wasn't an option for them.

Every fiber of her was on fire. How long had it been since she'd been properly kissed like that? Her insides liquefied, from the tip of her tongue down, sending searing heat to the valley of her nether areas. With just one swoop, he could easily lift her onto the counter. And she knew if she didn't stop this, she would allow him.

Thinking logically, Macy pressed her hand against his broad chest. She couldn't do this, not now. She cleared her throat. "Um, speaking of Serena, I wonder if she's okay."

Just as Duke raised an eyebrow, the phone next to the utility desk rang to the tune of "Jingle Bells." Macy took just a few steps to catch it on the second ring. "Hello." She leaned against the desk and watched Duke's amused face.

"You jinxed me!" Serena croaked on the other end of the line.

Macy balanced the phone on her shoulder, closed her eyes and crossed her fingers. "*I wish I'd win the lottery. I wish I'd win the lottery*," she chanted, and then picked the phone up again, ignoring Duke's quizzical expression. His eyebrows went up in surprise and his lips threatened to emit a laugh, turning up at the corners.

"Oh my God. I knew my ears were burning. I'm dying here and you're talking about me?" wailed Serena, sounding congested, stuffy and sneezy. Macy didn't have to guess to add "feverish." Perhaps this wasn't one of Serena's tricks of trying to set her up with a single client.

Covering the phone, Macy mouthed to Duke that she was speaking with her assistant. The break was obviously needed for him, as well. He moved over to the sink, turning his back on her, and braced himself with his hands on either side of the sink. "No, we were just wondering how you were doing."

"Mr. Dimples showed up?"

"Of course." Macy hid her smile and turned around. "Everything will be fine here. You take care of yourself, and I'll be over later with some soup for you."

"Please don't kill him, Macy. I love him."

Chuckling, Macy nodded. Her body was still vibrating from the electrifying kiss. "I won't."

"And when I get better, you can thank me."

"For?" Macy glanced at the speaker part of her phone.

"For letting you spend time with your celebrity crush." Serena disconnected from the line before Macy got the chance to respond. She turned back to face Duke with Serena's words lingering in her mind. Her celebrity crush had kissed her. She touched the pad of her thumb to her bottom lip and almost let out a schoolgirl giggle. A *clink* from the sink brought her to reality. Duke had managed quietly to wash out their mugs and set them in the adjoining sink.

"You didn't have to do that," she said.

"I didn't mind." He turned around and leaned against the sink, mocking her pose. Their feet almost met in the center of the kitchen but didn't touch. "It was the closest way of giving you privacy, so that your assistant can tell you to be nice to me." He wiggled his eyebrows up and down, teasing her. "I'd say you're off to a nice start."

Macy could feel herself blush before she could open her mouth. Her cheeks tingled. "Look, that type of thing can't happen again."

"What thing?"

"The kissing." She cleared her throat in an attempt to sound professional. "I don't make it a habit of kissing my employees."

Duke nodded and looked down at her feet. He tapped her toe with the tip of his boot. "You do realize that I'm not really an employee of yours."

"I know. But we have to work together over the next few days…"

"I haven't figured out when I'm going to throw the party, so it might take weeks."

"Well then, weeks. Either way, getting involved is not a good idea," she said, squaring her shoulders and standing up straight. Weeks? She was going to have to spend more time with him than expected. Being around a man who could kiss like that and had professed his desire for her… Macy shook her head, not knowing how she was going to be able to resist him.

Slowly, he stood up and nodded. "Are you involved with someone?"

"No!" she exclaimed, appalled that he would think she would just kiss someone if she were involved. "I'm single."

"Are you not attracted to me?"

She closed her mouth as quickly as she opened it and searched for a logical answer. "Well, I'm not going to say that you're not attractive."

"I think there was a compliment in there." As he

smiled and licked his lips, she couldn't help but watch, recalling how that same exact tongue had just grazed hers. Her heart raced when he pushed himself away from the counter and moved closer to her. She craned her neck, promising herself not to budge. He was a good six inches taller than her. He placed his hands on either side of the desk, trapping her. The dimple in his cheek deepened when he grinned. *Mr. Dimples.*

"Maybe there was. Do I think you're good-looking? Sure. But so does half the world." Macy kept her breath steady, despite her fast-beating heart, and prayed she sounded as nonchalant as she tried to make herself sound. "I just know you're not going to be here long, and I think that starting something that can't be finished is a ridiculous thing to do. I have responsibilities, children, work…" She ticked off more things that she had to do while he stroked the side of her face with the back of his fingers.

"I think that all depends on what your definition of finishing is. Are you looking to get married?"

"God, no!" she blurted out.

"Are you looking for a live-in boyfriend or something?"

She shook her head no.

"Then it just depends on two people's definition of spending time together."

"We barely know each other," Macy heard herself say. Did she say it, or was it more of a plea? Either way, it was a ridiculous thing to come out of her mouth, especially when her heart was speeding up, knowing he was going to kiss her again. And she was going to let him. She closed her eyes as he lowered his lips to hers and kissed her softly.

"I can't help but feel like I know you. I like talking to you." He moved his mouth by her earlobe. She knew she should protest, but it just felt so damn nice to be touched this way.

"Why do you want to get to know me?"

"I'm infatuated with you, Macy Cuomo." He rested his forehead against hers and looked into her eyes. "I haven't stopped thinking about you since I saw you in the foyer of the Baez home. Would I like nothing more than to forget about this day and place you on this counter and make love to you all day? Yes. But I know you're a woman who takes her work seriously."

Had he known that same thought ran wickedly through her mind just a few minutes ago? His bold honesty scared her. She shivered. "Infatuations come and go."

"But isn't it fun discovering each other along the way? What harm could come from going out to eat?"

Macy inhaled deeply. "I have a Thanksgiving meal we can eat together when we're done working."

"So then dinner is a good start."

"Just dinner?"

"I'm a forty-year-old man, Macy. Just having a quick roll in the hay is over and done with for me. Can't we get to know each other? If you find you're not attracted to me, just think, my contract with WKSS is up in a few weeks, and you won't have to deal with me."

"Oh, how romantic," Macy said with a droll eye roll.

However, how often did a woman have an opportunity to kiss her celebrity crush?

"I just want to be around you." He kissed her again; this time, he trailed his lips along her chin and down her throat to the crook of her neck. The backs of her knees began to sweat.

"Yet you keep kissing me."

He pulled away with a tight smile and pointed his finger upward. "Then you might want to stop standing underneath the mistletoe."

Chapter 4

For once, outing Santa had worked in Duke's favor. After coming home from Pablo's party, Duke had found college kids toilet-papering his front lawn. The two guys sang like canaries, confessing they sought revenge for their boss, Macy Cuomo, who'd come into work pissed off about him exposing Santa as a fraud on television. Instead of calling the cops, Duke had used the situation to work in his favor and bought the frat boys off, sending them down to Miami on an all-expenses-paid football vacation. And he wasn't the slightest bit sorry.

Duke rapped his knuckles against the bright red door of the Winter Paradise office and leaned in close to try to hear Macy coming down the stairs. How was it possible his knuckles ached? Who knew manning a staple gun required such a steady hand? A day hanging up

Christmas lights beat a two-week training session at a top-notch gym. His thighs burned from climbing up and down Macy's narrow red twenty-four-foot ladder.

"Good morning," Macy sang, yanking the door open and closing it quickly behind her. The naughty Santa behind her called out his usual *ho-ho-ho* greeting.

Because she closed the door so quickly, Duke did not get the chance to step backward, so Macy stood pressed between him and the door. He contemplated pinning her against the door and showing her what a good morning it already was.

"Good morning," he finally breathed, taking a moment to appreciate her exposed legs in a pair of tiny shorts. Her smooth stems spilled into a pair of low-top pink canvas shoes, and her hair was pulled high in a ponytail on top of her head. The white shirt she wore reminded Duke of one of his old baseball tees, with pink for the sleeves and rim of the collar. His heart slammed against his rib cage and his palms began to sweat. *Maybe it's the heat*, he thought. Yesterday the weather started off cool, and by midmorning, the skies had turned very summery. Getting used to the Thanksgiving holiday being so warm was going to take some time, but the sight of Macy in a pair of shorts, tennis shoes and thin top was something to help ease his mind.

Macy hiked her purse onto her shoulder and worked her way around him and down the steps. Turning her face up toward his, she smiled and blinked, fluttering her long lashes. "Are you ready?"

The porch light highlighted her face. Duke enjoyed a woman who didn't cake makeup on with a shovel. High-definition television drove a lot of women to all sorts of crazy facial antics. When his television-personality ex, Kristina Barclay, traveled, she carried her own luggage filled with makeup. As a television personality, Duke occasionally endured a powder puff here and there, usually after fighting the artists tooth and nail. Macy just wore some mascara and lip gloss. Her long lashes framed her light brown eyes. Her lips were tempting enough to kiss again as he had yesterday, but the last thing he wanted to do was scare her off. After his blatant confession about his infertility hadn't scared her off, he thought he might actually have a chance.

Duke did not like the idea of comparing Kristina and Macy. He and Kristina meshed because they both wanted the same thing out of life—success. While his father was the most influential man in his life, Duke never wanted to travel the same farmer's path. He knew his family had sacrificed quite a few luxury items such as braces, dresses—even getting the family car fixed— in order to send him to baseball camp, which was what kept Duke striving harder to succeed. He owed it to his family.

Making good on his debt hadn't been hard for Duke. He'd been enamored by the rich lifestyle of the scouts who came over to watch him play ball. He wanted the fancy car and a passport stamped from countries around the world. Being able to come and go without any romantic responsibility in life dazzled him. He'd seen his college teammates settle down with a family before graduation, limiting their dreams, and Duke did not want the same. He liked his fast cars and to come and go whenever he wanted. Kristina had never expected anything more from Duke. She found his inability to have children a blessing. Before Kristina, the women Duke dated hinted that they wanted a family. Some even tried to trap him by claiming to be pregnant. Knowing he would not have children of his own had never bothered him until now.

Being around Macy gave him a glimpse of what life would be like if he slowed down. He felt nothing but good vibes looking at the family photos and school projects hanging on the walls and refrigerator of Macy's business kitchen. Growing up in Mao, his mother had decorated her refrigerator with his accolades. Meanwhile, the subzero fridge in his condo in DC remained bare. In fact, the factory seal might still be on it, which reminded Duke something was missing in his life. But until he figured it out, slowing down had never felt good.

Last night probably had to have been the highlight of his time in Tallahassee—maybe the highlight all year. There was no need for a fancy restaurant; Macy's meal in Tupperware dishes she'd set aside for her two workers was superb. When they'd finished with the last house, Macy invited Duke in to share a small meal and watch some television. She said it was somewhat of a tradition with her employees.

He looked down at the woman in front of him and had to grin. He thought of all the women he'd known in his life, and by far none of them had impressed him like Macy Cuomo.

"Not that I'm complaining about looking at your gorgeous legs, but aren't you a bit underdressed for climbing rooftops?" His head turned in typical male fashion and smiled appreciatively at her backside as she waltzed down her brick walkway. Her shorts hugged the curves of her hips. Duke followed her to the side of the house where she kept her Jeep.

"We're not doing any decorating just yet," she called over her shoulder, opening a door. "We're doing a little shopping."

She cast an innocent smile. Her doe eyes fluttered at him. Duke had done enough Black Friday segments that he knew there was nothing "little" about shopping today. He stood his ground and waited for the engine of the automatic garage door to quiet down after opening up. "You know, studies have shown that the best day to get deals is actually Christmas Eve."

"What?"

"I'm just saying, you're not going to find the best deals today. Don't you want to relax?"

With her hand on the door of her red pickup Jeep, Macy shook her head and laughed at him. "If you can't hang, you are more than welcome to go back inside. I have a hideaway key underneath the Christmas deer's hoof by the front door. I'll let you know when I'm pulling up and you can help me with my bags." Before she got in the truck, Duke swore he saw her smiling. He liked it.

Duke cast a glance back at the Christmas-decorated lawn. Unlike the other lawns they'd worked on, hers was subtle. A few lighted deer casually grazed on the grass. Simple white lights trimmed the roof of the house, as well as the picket fence. He shook his head and grinned as she backed her vehicle into the driveway and rolled down the window. Duke came over and leaned against the driver's-side window. "So you just want to use me for my muscle, eh?" To add to the joke, he flexed his biceps.

Macy shook her head and laughed. "Let's see if we can get those twigs built up before the holiday season is over."

For the most part, Macy presented herself as all work and no play. All day yesterday, he thought the kiss between them must have been a mere fluke, but just now when she bit the corner of her bottom lip and batted her lashes, he knew better.

Duke opened the door on his side and hopped in. "Let's hit the roads. Today *is* one of the busiest shopping days of the year."

"Don't worry," she said with a wink, "I've earned myself a place at the front of all the lines."

He half laughed. "That's funny, because with my puny arms I seem to get to the front of all the lines, too."

Macy walked through the aisles of major stores like a celebrity; salesmen followed her aimlessly with large flats, grabbing and reaching for everything she pointed at and said she wanted. Shopping with Macy was interesting, to say the least. Duke was completely unprepared for it.

At noon, they stopped and had lunch. Duke insisted they sit down and take a break from the hustle and bustle. Macy chose a small bistro called Nicole's. The restaurant was pleasantly placed just outside Lake Ella, which was near the downtown area. Together, they dined, seated across from each other at a wrought-iron table with a green umbrella shading them from the afternoon sun. Ducks quacked on the water, while children ran toward the edge to throw whole pieces of bread into the lake. Duke took a long drink of his sweet tea.

"Tired yet?" Macy taunted him.

He had yet to see her break a sweat. Meanwhile, his feet were hurting. "No."

It was a lie. He knew it. She knew it.

Slowly she smiled, held her red straw between her fingers and guided it toward her glossy lips. "It's okay if you are. I'm surprised you haven't crashed by now."

"I don't see how you do it." Duke sighed in relief and relaxed against his chair.

Macy shrugged her shoulders. "It's a lot easier when my kids are with their father. Otherwise, I'm dragging them around with me and putting them to work." She held her hand in the air before he could even think to say anything. "And before you say anything, yes, Gia is old enough to watch MJ, but if I left them alone, then my cell phone would ring off the hook over the two of them fighting."

"I had a hard time getting my brothers and sisters to listen to me when we were growing up."

"How many do you have?"

"I have three brothers who are older than me—Bobby, Sandino and Erik. They live in the States. And then my two younger sisters, Ana and Theresa, both live back home near my folks."

"So your folks are still alive?"

"Yeah." Duke stretched, not sure how comfortable Macy was talking about parents, considering she'd lost hers in the bombing attacks when she was a teenager. "My parents still get around. One of these days I'm going to get them to come to the States for the holidays. Tell me more about your kids. MJ's eight, so that's what? Second grade?"

He liked that she beamed when she spoke of her kids. Her face lit up like a Christmas tree. Her dark eyes softened, and any trace of tiredness was gone. Her cheeks gave a slight hint of pink as she blushed.

"Third. And Gia is in ninth grade."

Duke winced. "Oh, sorry. I remember when my sisters went through high school."

He still recalled their tears due to rejection from boyfriends; the mood swings were just teenage angst. There was also the embarrassment Ana and Theresa had dealt with, not only from their parents, but their brothers, as well.

"Should I assume they were sweet little girls until they hit high school?"

"Exactly. But it's all about knowing how to talk to kids." Duke relaxed in his seat.

Their waitress arrived with their lunches. Macy had ordered the grouper sandwich with seasoned fries, which sounded so wonderful Duke got the same. They ate quietly for a few minutes, just enough time to satisfy their hunger, and then Macy cleared her throat. He was glad for that, because he liked a woman who could carry on a conversation.

"So with your vast experience with kids, teenagers in particular, you think you know how to handle them?" She was playing coy. A dimple popped out in her cheek when she tried not to grin at him.

"Of course. I think kids just appreciate honesty."

"Like outing Santa?" she interjected with a lopsided smirk and a raised eyebrow.

He bowed his head for a moment and then lifted his eyes toward hers. She'd bitten the corner of her lip again. "I'm sorry that slipped out. You know I wouldn't do something that cruel on purpose."

"Mmm-hmm." He eyed her suspiciously. The more she sat grinning at him with her Cheshire Cat smile, the more he wanted to lean over and kiss her.

Kissing her yesterday had kept him fueled during the day and night. His body had been so wired from spending time with her that he barely slept. He'd actually tossed and turned in his bed last night until he just lay on his back with his hands behind his head and thought about her lips against his.

"Seriously, if I have to re-create the North Pole myself, I will do so if it means helping you prove to MJ that Santa still exists." He reached across the table and touched the back of her hand. Her skin was soft, like the petal of a rose.

Macy scoffed and rolled her eyes, but didn't move her hand. "No need to go all extreme. As a matter of fact, you don't have to keep working with me if you don't want."

Every time she got nervous, she came up with one excuse or another to let him out of his obligation. Yesterday, he'd foolishly hit his hand with a hammer while tacking up lights, and she tried to let him off the hook. The truth was, he'd been so preoccupied with their last kiss that he hadn't been paying attention.

As the traffic around them grew louder with the afternoon shoppers, Duke squeezed Macy's hand slightly. "Will you stop trying to offer me a way out of this arrangement? I said I am helping."

"Yes, but that was so I could do your house. I'm just saying, I'll still do your house."

"You don't seem to get it."

"Get what?"

"You don't seem to have time any other way, so this is my selfish method of getting to spend time with you." He thought she would eventually figure that one out.

After a minute of his hand resting on hers, Macy conceded and nodded her head. "I supposed I should be grateful for your help. I can't believe Andy and Spencer would bail on me. I know that Serena is sick…so I guess I *should* stop."

Duke hid his smile at her reluctant "should." Either way, Duke didn't mind. He let go of her hand and sat back, smiling like the cat that ate the canary. He knew he should have felt guilty for buying off Andy and Spencer, but he didn't. He had Macy all to himself.

"Have you thought about when you want to have your party and who you want to invite?"

"What about Christmas Eve?" Duke picked up his drink, pushed the straw out of the way and sipped from the cup. Macy did the same. He liked that she didn't look at him with such hate, like she had the first time they'd spoken. He wanted all the folks at the WKSS studio, as well as the viewers he'd pissed off, to accept his apology. In Mao, having a village party took little effort, so why not do the same here? "And I want to invite everyone."

She half choked on her drink. "Everyone?"

"Yes, I'm going to announce it on the morning news this week. I wanted to discuss it with you."

"Duke, your party is going to cost a fortune."

"Money is no object, and I want the house to be really festive, so whatever you want to charge me, have at it."

"That's three weeks away."

"Do you need more time?"

He liked the way she pressed her lips together when she was in thought. "No, we can do it."

Duke gave her a devilish smile and grin. Macy rolled her eyes, but her cheeks flushed. When was the last time someone had openly flirted with her? A gorgeous woman like her…men surely threw themselves at her feet left and right.

"I mean the party," Macy quickly clarified. "What kinds of food do you want?"

"Whatever you think would be good." He shrugged, not caring about the food or the cost of things. The only thing that mattered to Duke was that he was spending more time with Macy, and he had three weeks to secure her presence at his party, not as his caterer and decorator, but as something more. Something much, much more. What? Duke didn't know. It dawned on him that he had no game plan here.

Macy was reluctant to get involved with him because he would be leaving after the New Year. But what kind of life would he return to? He hated the fact that his personal life was displayed in the tabloids. Prior to Kristina, he never thought of marriage. Though his parents had been happily married for what seemed like an eternity, there was more to life than marriage—or so Duke thought.

Kristina had proposed to him in more of a business-like manner. Like Duke, she'd attended college in South Florida. They both wanted to conquer the media world. He never imagined they'd be what the viewers called a power couple. Late last spring, after celebrating at a successful music award show, Kristina laid out her proposal, including all the endorsements they'd receive for product placements as a married couple, and she already had a date set for when they'd adopt a child and introduce it on a special report. At the time, he had no idea how to answer her.

Truthfully, the whole idea sickened him. His parents married for love, not business. His father made a grand scheme of a proposal to Duke's mother. Without being able to provide the potential for a child, Duke felt a proposal should at least be his decision. He hated not having control of his life, from the trainers who kept him fit to the ladies at the studios who chose his wardrobe. Feeling powerless scared him. And he'd taken a leave of absence from the DC news desk and headed down to Mao for some soul searching and got caught up with the baseball training camps back in the DR. The temporary break from the news desk and the permanent break from Kristina would change his world if he went back.

If? Funny how his "when" turned into an "if" now, he thought. A few weeks ago, he couldn't wait for the day when he got a late-night phone call with a story breaking. Now his mindset was a bit more relaxed. If he decided to renew his contract, he wasn't sure it would be with the DC affiliate. At work, there was always someone picking out his clothes. Thanks to a trainer who kept him fit, he remained in the magazines as a sex symbol. He always had someone to keep him on track.

There was something about Macy, Duke thought as he shifted in his seat. What he liked about her was the refreshing way she dealt with him. She gave him a task and allowed him to complete it without handling him with kid gloves. She gave him what he'd sought after for a while. She treated him like a man.

He got simple joy from just being around her. She was refreshing. She was entertaining. He enjoyed being around a woman who didn't count every calorie before it entered her mouth. He liked that when they were shopping, she didn't dictate orders to everyone around her. People seemed to follow her every whim because they genuinely liked her, not because they were scared of her. Kristina demanded fear from everyone. She may have not wanted Duke for his money or for a family, like other women he'd dated, but she did crave attention. The more, the better.

"Is everything okay with your food?" the waitress asked, rushing over to the table. She'd already come by for a picture and an autograph, and had him speak with her grandmother on the phone, who seemed to be in love with him.

Kristina would have called the manager over and had the woman fired by now. Macy sat back and grinned the entire time; she'd even made a sarcastic joke here and there each time the waitress came over with something new, but it was never anything malicious, just a joke on him. Duke realized he must have been frowning. The thought of Kristina did that to him. He pushed his plate away, folded his hands across his lap and smiled. "Yes, thank you. Everything is just perfect."

After she left, Macy was still looking at him. "You *were* frowning," she confirmed with a raised eyebrow.

"Sorry, I didn't mean to."

Macy sat back in her seat and folded her hands in her lap just as he had. The sun hit her face, lighting her chocolate-brown eyes. Her skin blended with the sun, making it golden. *Damn, she is beautiful*, Duke thought to himself.

"You know, I recognize that frown. You were thinking of an ex, weren't you?"

Duke knew better than to answer. But he wasn't going to lie to her. She didn't even seem bothered by it; she just asked the question the way a friend would. "I'd rather not say."

"That's probably wise," Macy mumbled, and then grinned. "But for whatever it is worth, you can work things out if you truly want."

He wanted Macy. Her attempt to sympathize with him was even more endearing. She was trying to give him hope that things could work out with Kristina. Perhaps his kisses didn't mean that much to her or just weren't sinking in. He leaned in closer. "If we're referring to what I think, trust me, I truly don't want things like that to work out."

"I can understand."

"You and your ex?" He knew she was married once before. He knew she had children with this man, and Duke didn't think of himself as the jealous type, but a part of him was glad that Macy's relationship hadn't worked out. Otherwise, this luncheon would have gone a completely different way. "How long have you been divorced?"

"Seven years divorced now, but we were the best of friends for the longest time before marriage," Macy shared with him.

"How did you two meet?" Duke thought the man had to be the world's biggest fool for letting her go.

"Both sets of my grandparents were friends with his parents, and they thought it would be cute to put us together because of our backgrounds. We each have a grandparent who migrated from Italy, so they insisted we attend the Sons and Daughters of Italy Club."

Duke didn't give a damn about Macy's background. A beautiful woman was a beautiful woman. In the DR, women came in every shade of color.

"We just knew we were destined to be friends."

As much as he hated to admit it, the thought of Macy still friends with an ex made him uncomfortable, unsure. He'd never felt that way before. Jealousy was not something he had in him. He used to think there were too many women in the world to get jealous, but then he met Macy. She was the only person he was concerned with right now.

When Duke took his initial break from the news desk, he'd done so with the blessing of the station production manager, Oscar Orsini. Oscar also produced Kristina's *Spotlight on Socialites* show. Without caring whether or not Duke accepted Kristina's business proposal of marriage, the two of them conspired together and planned out the Rodriguez/Barclay wedding; the list of sponsors and endorsements had taken over three pages in an email. Still with no idea how to say no to Kristina, Duke returned to DC and found out exactly why Oscar and Kristina were spending so much time together. Duke had guessed that, with his absence and lack of response, an affair between the two must have been foreseeable. This time, when Duke left DC, Oscar accepted his open-ended leave of absence.

How Macy's ex could just be friends with her was beyond him. He couldn't imagine watching her go out with a different man. And that was after only one kiss. He couldn't imagine how he would feel after making love to her.

"I doubt I can be friends with…"

"Kristina?"

He wanted to tell Macy he wasn't sure he could be just friends with *her*, not Kristina. But instead of telling her what he was thinking, he just cleared his throat. It didn't surprise him that Macy had heard of Kristina. He'd tried as much as he could to keep private life private; stories got out.

Since he'd been away from the limelight in DC, he

hadn't had that problem as much, and it was refreshing. When he played baseball, he was used to reporters asking him questions after a game, but when he became an anchorman himself, it almost seemed as if he was stalked every time he went out with Kristina. The more he thought about it, the more he realized Kristina could have easily phoned in their whereabouts.

"I really can't see Kristina and me being friends, just because we have nothing in common."

"Is that why you two broke up?" Macy asked and then quickly shook her head. "I'm sorry. I shouldn't have asked such a personal question."

Relaxing in his chair, Duke chuckled. Macy could ask him anything in the world. Considering he'd already told Macy about his infertility, why not go ahead and blab about Kristina's infidelity? But he did not want to come off as wounded. The tabloids already speculated a breakup, along with a graph of how many events Kristina attended alone. It was only a matter of time before the truth came out. He just didn't want to bring that drama here. "It's okay. I haven't spoken about the situation. Without divulging too much, let's just say that we had a difference of opinion." He held back a grin when she started to nod her head in understanding and reached for her tea. She was on the edge of her seat, clearly waiting to hear the whole story. The whole world had been on the edge of its seat.

"She wanted to get married, didn't she?"

Duke had left DC first and as a result, the media pegged him as the bad guy. Typically, he didn't care what people thought about him. As long as he knew the truth, he was okay with what others thought. But today it was different. It affected Macy's view of him.

"Yes, she wanted to get married, but not for the reasons you may think. In her eyes, we were this power couple in the news."

"You guys did rival Jay-Z and Beyoncé or Brad and Angelina for a while in the media," Macy chimed in with a cocky smile. "Not like I paid attention or anything."

"You're good for my ego." Duke clutched his heart and wobbled to the side a bit in jest. "The whole media thing was not my idea. I wanted something low-key. Believe it or not, I like the idea of an intimate relationship, one that's not plastered over the gossip tabloids."

Slowly Macy nodded her head as if she understood. He doubted she did. No one did. "Yet you continued the relationship with her?"

"I just went with the flow of things. But we had different ways of getting ahead in life. I thought journalism meant getting the story by any means necessary. I just never thought sleeping with someone to get a story was the way to go."

Obviously he'd surprised her with the revelation. Her mouth opened to a perfect O. "I thought…" She let her words trail.

"You guessed I strayed?" Duke asked with a raised eyebrow.

"Well, uh," she stammered, her light eyes averted toward the condensation sweating from the glass of tea. "You do have that bad-boy quality about you. And when the news of the two of you breaking up hit, you were seen with a bunch of different women."

He'd been told that before. He knew. His history as a baseball player allowed him to behave in what would be considered a bad-boy way. But he was in his twenties then. He'd grown. Just because there was a woman in every zip code waiting to give herself to him didn't mean he had to act upon it.

"I can admit that the way I handled myself wasn't the right way, but I quickly was reminded that my bad-boy streak in life was over."

"May I ask who reminded you?"

"My sister Ana." Duke cleared his throat, not proud of himself, but he had this feeling that Macy wasn't going to judge him. "I was in a hotel when she called me on my cell phone and asked if I knew the name of the woman lying next to me. And when I didn't, she asked how I would feel if some guy didn't remember her name."

Macy covered her mouth and sat back. Her eyes narrowed on him. He winced inwardly, praying that she wasn't judging him. "So then you left?"

"More or less. Pablo called me soon after I talked to my sister. He reminded me also about how I said I wanted a relationship. I actually always saw myself settling down with just one woman, kind of like my folks. And I envy Pablo's married life with Mo."

Macy nodded her head in agreement. "They are a great couple."

"I think so. I mean, I knew them both in college, and I can't say I've ever seen two people so perfectly suited for each other." He shrugged at his own honesty. "I always wanted a good woman on my arm, someone who made me realize my priorities but still loved me for my imperfections. You know, the kind of woman you would do anything for."

"That sounds very romantic, Duke."

"I'm a very romantic guy. Just give me a chance," he countered.

Picking up her glass, she visibly hid her smile. "After you just told me you went through a slew of women after you got your heart broken?"

"That's cold, Macy." Duke blew out a low whistle and shook his head. "She didn't break my heart."

"But you guys were engaged."

"Yeah, but…"

"Didn't you want to marry her?"

Maybe she should have been the reporter with her rapid, on-point questions. He liked that Macy didn't candy-coat things. She challenged him. "No, I didn't. But it didn't mean I appreciated being deceived, either."

Her eyes diverted to the ground and then moved back at up to him. "Sorry."

"It's okay." He shrugged. "In a way, it was a blessing in disguise."

"How do you figure?"

"Because it led me here."

He liked it when she blushed again. She tucked a strand of hair behind her ear with her fingers.

"So, are you going to give me a chance?"

Blushing, she rolled her eyes skyward. "What is it you want from me?"

"It depends on your definition of *want*," he began as

she raised her eyebrows in question. So he followed up with a reply. "In DC, I didn't really have time to date around."

"Sounds like you got around enough," she interjected quickly before clamping her hand over her mouth. "Sorry!" she added with a playful giggle.

"Anyway, being a journalist, I never had time to do the typical dating thing. I would have to cover one event or another. Kristina, I guess, was convenient to date and understanding, since she was a reporter, as well. Our schedules matched."

Macy nodded and took another sip of her drink. Just seeing her lips move over her glass made his body stir. He readjusted the way he sat so that he wouldn't make it so visibly obvious how much he wanted her. "Makes sense," Macy was saying. "My schedule for dating has been a bit off-kilter."

"So you're saying you haven't been on a date in a while?"

"Ah, let's see." She tilted her head back, giving him a glance of her beautiful neck, sculpted just for his lips. He cleared his throat, hoping it would settle the stirring in his pants, but it didn't. "I went out a few times with this one man for lunch. Does that count?"

"It depends. What does he do for a living?"

"He's a pilot."

"A pilot?" he asked. Macy didn't strike him as the type of woman who went for flyboys. Of course, she also didn't strike him as the type to go for former athletes, either, especially because of the special word she called him. There had to have been another reason. "Were you talking about work?"

Duke wanted to know if she'd kissed the pilot, but refrained from asking. He didn't want to know. He didn't want to think of some other man making her squirm as he did yesterday.

"His house won first place last year in his neighborhood."

"Then you didn't date him. He was a client. If he was a smart pilot, he would have flown you to another city for lunch."

"So what do you have in mind? I bet you can't think of much, now that you're in slowpoke Tallahassee."

"Tallahassee's not so bad," he said honestly. The weather was different, especially for this time of year, but prior to his outing Santa, the people had been friendly. And then of course, there was Macy.

"How do you like it?"

Duke leaned back in his chair and smiled appreciatively at her beautiful face. Just looking at her made him grin. Her smile challenged him. He couldn't use any line as he could on another woman, and he wouldn't want to on her. "I have to admit, I've absolutely fallen in love with this town."

The same reddening flush from earlier reappeared at Macy's cheeks. "I see."

The fact that she clearly tried as hard as she could to resist him affected him. Duke had to shift in his seat and remind himself that he was a grown man, not a boy easily aroused by a smile, but there was just something about Macy. "Do you? Do you really?"

In an apparent attempt to change the subject, Macy cleared her throat, but Duke leaned in closer and took her hand again. "I know you may think it's soon, Macy, but I can tell by the way you react every time I touch you, you're just as curious about where things can go between us."

"I—I..." She fumbled for words and stuttered.

"I am just asking for you give me a chance." He leaned closer and pressed his lips against hers. She tasted sweet like tea, but he knew she had her own sweetness. He had tasted it yesterday and had to abstain from taking more. Macy was the type of person who needed to take things slow. He respected the fact she had two children. As a matter of fact, he couldn't wait to meet them. But in the meantime, images of making love to her flooded his mind. The feel of her mouth made his body pulsate. It was all he could do to keep from taking her on the table right now. But he knew he couldn't.

People from nearby tables oohed and ahhed at the two of them, and a few of them even clapped. Macy pulled away for a split second, and then her body melted into his, just as it had done yesterday. Her hands clasped the sides of his face as she pulled him closer to her. She was an expert kisser. If they weren't in public, Duke would have pushed everything and acted on impulse. His heart slammed against his rib cage. A car horn sounded behind them, and though he was sure he wasn't the cause of it, he heard tires screech against the street.

Pictures formed in his head: Macy and his mother standing in the kitchen talking and laughing. Picturing his mother while he was kissing Macy wasn't ideal. But he thought it meant something. That kind of domesticity, something he'd never pictured before, especially not while kissing a woman. Reluctantly he pulled away.

He liked the way her long eyelashes fluttered as she tried to come back into focus. When she did, she blinked and smiled shyly. "Mmm-kay."

Chapter 5

Birthdays in his childhood had always been a big event, Duke reminisced, pulling his Ferrari into the circular driveway of Macy's ranch-style home off Mistletoe Court for her birthday celebration. The family didn't have a lot of money growing up, but they always had a good time. Family and friends would come from miles away to eat and then head out to swim on the beach. Many would spend the night, which was already cramped with three brothers and two sisters having to share two rooms. The girls, of course, had their own room, but the male cousins slept in his room, thus making it impossible to walk across the floor in the middle of the night to go to the bathroom.

Duke pressed his lips together, impressed with Macy's style of home. From what he'd learned, she used to live in the office of Winter Paradise. It was easy to see how that Victorian-style house had been a home and how it turned into her place of business. Her new house was quite impressive itself. He'd prefer a spread like hers for himself one day. Once Duke had graduated from high school and didn't have to live with his siblings, he thought he would always want his own spread. Living in New York and DC hadn't helped him see his dream come true, but being down south certainly had opened his eyes for him.

The ranch-style home sat on a large piece of property far from the curb. At one end, the garage connected to the outside porch, which was lined with three rocking chairs on one side and a hanging swing on the other. On the side where the garage door was, there were four large windows decorated with a trim of white lights. Near the end where the swing was stood a bay window with a dressed Christmas tree.

When Macy reminded Duke this morning on the phone about her small party, she failed to clarify how many people were coming. What Macy defined as an intimate gathering turned out to be at least a dozen cars or so parked in her driveway, street and lawn. When she had originally asked him over, Duke was under the impression she'd invited her family, maybe Pablo and Monique. Judging from the cars parked outside, he doubted he'd be able to get any alone time with Macy. As disappointing as that was, he was still eager just to be under the same roof as her. Before getting out of the car, he reached into the backseat for the rectangular box, perfectly wrapped in a light pink. He'd discovered over the past few days that her favorite color was, surprisingly, pink. With her job, he would have half expected Macy to like red and green. The contents of the small box rattled. A smile tugged at his lips. He couldn't wait to see her face when she opened it.

As his foot hit the first step, he heard a group of girls screaming from upstairs. He reached for the doorbell, but before he could pull his finger away the door jerked open. Duke straightened to his full height and flashed his award-winning, camera-ready smile.

"Duke Rodriguez, well damn, ain't this something. I've been a fan of yours for quite a while," exclaimed a stocky man with arms big enough to bench press his Ferrari. He was close to six feet tall, but not by much. What he might have lacked in height, he made up in muscle. The man must have been a professional body-builder. "I'm Mario Polizzi."

Duke extended his hand, swearing privately this man was trying to break his hand for no reason…then he quickly made the connection. "Oh, Macy's…" He couldn't bring himself to say "ex-husband." This man was obviously more of a meathead than someone who was smart enough to hang on to a woman like Macy. Mario's loss was his gain. Duke smiled and gave his hand a firmer shake. "It's a pleasure to meet you."

Releasing the viselike grip, Mario smiled broadly and his dark hooded eyes lightened up as he grinned. "I'm really glad you came over today. I've heard so much about you…*ow-ow-ow*."

Mario's face suddenly twisted in a cringe; his eyes squinted and his mouth tightened as if to keep from cursing. Duke couldn't imagine anything would cause the man pain. Didn't he work out every single day? Duke checked out his muscles popping out from his blue tank top. Not only did he have one of those barbed-wire tattoos across his biceps, but there was also a much smaller hand pulling the hairs on his arm. Duke couldn't see who the hand belonged to, but he had an idea.

Mario shook his head. "I'm sorry," he said in a robotic tone, "I've never heard anything about you before in my life." His eyes widened and stretched while his head nodded to whoever it was behind the door. Duke caught the hint.

"Well, it's a pleasure to meet you either way. Polizzi. Related to any of the Polizzis in DC?"

"So because I'm Italian, I gotta know everyone whose last name begins with a consonant?"

Duke opened his mouth to apologize, but when he did he saw the hand on Mario's arm pull the hair again. "Ow, ow, ow." Mario winced, his eyes visibly watering, but then he playfully punched the air just a fraction before Duke's ribs. "I'm just messin' with you!"

"So I heard there's someone here who knows a little bit about journalism. Someone named Gia?"

"Oh my God, he knows your name!" squealed a squeaky, girlie voice from behind the door.

The door pulled open wider and Duke came face-to-face with a mini replica of Macy. He now knew exactly what Macy looked like as a young girl—all legs, hair and big brown eyes.

"Gia, honey, this is Duke Rodriguez. Duke, this is my daughter, Gia, the aspiring reporter."

Frozen like a deer caught in the headlights, Gia stared at Duke. There was a slight sound of "hi" or "hello" that came out of her mouth, and then her two friends flanking her grabbed her hands and pulled her up the stairs. Behind the closed doors, he could hear their screams.

"Did I do something wrong?" Duke asked Mario.

Mario reached into his back pocket and extracted a black cell phone. "I'll tell ya in a second. C'mon in. Can I get you a beer?"

"A beer sounds good."

"So you're an alcoholic?"

Duke did a double take. "What?"

Mario's face spread out in a smile. Duke recalled the photographs of young MJ on the office refrigerator. He definitely saw the connection. Mario made the same punching gesture toward Duke's ribs and laughed. "Aw, I'm just messin' with you."

"Mario, get away from him," Macy said, coming from down the hallway. She was dressed in a beige strapless sundress that reached down to the floor. Her thick curly hair framed her face; images of running his fingers through it entered his mind. Duke noticed her shoulders were bare, but for a gold crucifix that hung around her neck. His mother would love her already, just knowing she was Catholic.

"Why are you answering my door? You're supposed to be gone." Playfully, Macy punched at Mario's beefy arm before she turned and smiled up at Duke. She stood on her tiptoes, and instinctively Duke leaned down. She kissed him delicately on his cheek. Her lips were soft.

The kiss was gentle, but he'd been thinking about her all morning long, so that was enough to send a stirring under his belt. "I'm sorry if he's trying to get to your head."

"I wouldn't try anything like that," Mario said, voice cracking. The phone in his hand chirped. "Hey, dude, you're totally on fleek."

"Mario!" Macy exclaimed.

In his defense Mario held up his phone in one hand and pointed at it with the other. "Hey, that's not me. Your daughter posted this on Twitter."

Macy took hold of Duke's arm and led him down the hallway toward the living room, to the left of the stairs where Gia and her friends disappeared. "You'll have to excuse Mario, and take him with a grain of salt," she said.

"You two seem to get along well," Duke replied.

"Please don't be fooled by our banter." Macy shrugged her shoulders. "His family and mine go way back."

"I think I recall you mentioning it." Duke hoped he came off nonchalant. "But now you two are friends, for the kids' sake."

"It's easier being friends." Macy laughed nervously. "We watched a lot of friends go through divorces, and their fighting tore their families apart. We're the happiest divorced couple you'll ever meet."

Where Macy's office downstairs was full of Christmas memorabilia, her new home was quite different. On one side, family portraits lined the hallway in black frames against the beige walls. The other side resembled a bar that overlooked the sunken living room, with no sign of Christmas coming.

He spied the Baezes and nodded their way, knowing he'd talk to them in a minute. Duke wanted to soak in Macy's family pictures. He noticed an old picture of Macy when she graduated from high school, the standard photograph of casting a glance over her bare shoulder. Her hair had been pulled up; she was as gorgeous then as she was now. There was a wedding picture of an Italian-looking man with bronze skin and a woman with a café-au-lait complexion; he immediately recognized them as Macy's parents. Macy had inherited her mother's thick curly hair and her father's almond-shaped eyes.

The hallway ended with the kitchen to the right and the living room to the left. The pictures on the wall ended as well, but from what Duke could gather from them, Macy still appeared to have had a normal upbringing with both sets of her grandparents. She at least did all the things typical American girls did, from amusement parks to horseback-riding lessons and camping trips. He liked the various captured moments of her kids growing up. "When Gia is good, she's his, but when she's bad, she belongs to me. Go figure," Macy was saying.

Slightly uncomfortable with the closeness between the two of them, Duke tried to laugh off their friendly banter. She did say that she and Mario were destined to be just friends. "She got a phone for her birthday over the summer," Macy was explaining as she led Duke into the spacious kitchen, "and half the time the only way we can know what's going on in her life is through her Tweets."

Being in the media, Duke was familiar with Twitter. He refused to let everyone know where he was and what he was doing 24/7. As far as he was concerned, there was only one person he'd share that information with. He glanced down at the birthday girl beside him and grinned. "I almost forgot—this is for you."

Macy took the pink package slowly and shook her head. She bit her bottom lip as she looked down at the bow on the top. Her slim fingers toyed with the edges. "You didn't have to get me anything."

"Sure I did. It's your birthday."

He knew she was going to protest. So he took it from her and set it on the round oak table in the corner of the kitchen. The island in the center of the kitchen was filled with several trays with meat ready for the grill— chicken, steak, hamburgers and hot dogs.

Macy and Duke faced each other. She still held his hand. He could see her chest rising up and down from nervousness—something he adored. She couldn't fake innocence. "You can open it later," he whispered into her ear. He deserved an award for not nibbling on her lobes right now. Every inch of his body told him to kiss her, but unfortunately someone interrupted them.

"Duke!"

In the living room, Duke saw Pablo seated next to his wife on an overstuffed beige couch. Pablo got up to shake his hand. Monique held on to baby Lucia and beamed at the sight of Macy's hand possessively wrapped around Duke's forearm as she led him into the sunken living room.

With his free arm, Duke extended his hand toward his friend. "*Hola, hermano*, how's everything?"

"Great. Great," Pablo said, shaking his hand. "Are you ready to get back to work in the morning? Or have you been loafing around and you won't be able to get up?"

"Oh, he's been up," Macy spoke up for him. Still holding on to the handshake, Pablo eyeballed Duke, who tried not to laugh. He knew at some point during this party he and Pablo were going to have to talk. He leaned over to kiss Monique properly on both cheeks, and then planted a kiss on Lucia's head. The baby was fast asleep.

Music played in the background. He thought he recognized a bit of *bachata*. No doubt Pablo had been a part of the music selection. When his generation was growing up, the elders dismissed the heavy guitar and bass music as a fad they prayed would go away, even going as far as banning it in some places. But like most things, the more the adults tried to stop something, the more kids flocked to it. Now it was widely accepted within their crowd of music lovers.

Through the sliding glass door, Duke spotted a few couples out on the sprawling back porch swaying to the beat of the music. Duke had the sudden urge to sweep Macy into his arms and dance with her. He would love to feel her hips against his as they danced. But maybe now was not the right time.

Monique leaned forward in her seat, careful not to

squish the baby. "So Duke, how do you like the morning show?"

"It's good. Refreshing," he answered honestly.

"I loved getting up and spreading the news. I know it hasn't been long since I've been on maternity leave, but I miss going out and getting the story," Monique said.

Duke looked over at Macy and explained what he knew. "When we were in college, Mo uncovered every news story possible."

"She did it to get close to me," Pablo boasted. "She covered all the sports, too. Mo may have endured a lot of baseball games, but it was really so she could get an interview with me."

Playfully, Monique pinched Pablo's arm. "He's half right," she said to Macy.

"Here you go, man." Mario came over to the group with a cold bottle of beer already opened.

Duke thanked Mario and took a sip. "Actually, to be honest with you, I haven't missed the investigative side of reporting."

"It'd probably be hard to be an undercover reporter," Mario piped in, "with you being a famous baseball player and then being on ESPN for so long."

Duke nodded and took another sip of his beer. But he couldn't lie. He couldn't go anywhere without someone bringing up his time with the Yankees or as a sports reporter. No one remembered his interviews with politicians or his reports on Middle Eastern leaders. His job in DC had covered everything from politics to the local limelight. He reached his goal, breaking the mold of a dumb jock. Duke wanted to be the face viewers watched on television and trusted to bring them the news. People related to him and remembered his sports career. Sometimes, it took extra time to keep his guests focused on the story at hand, rather than reminiscing over past games. "My previous careers have had their drawbacks."

"Sit down, Duke," Macy said, fanning her hand toward the couch opposite Pablo and Monique. They fell into the cushions at the same time. Their hips touched, causing Macy to giggle slightly and adjust herself so she could look at him. As he looked into her eyes, it seemed like the rest of the world had been shut out. Duke leaned in closer and pressed his forehead against hers.

"Thank you for coming," she said quietly as she leaned over.

"You know I wouldn't have missed it for the world." Out of the corner of his eye, Duke didn't miss Monique elbowing Pablo in the ribs when he sat down.

"So Macy," Monique began, "how's your new helper coming along?"

Macy glanced up at Duke and beamed. "He's turning out to be not as pampered as I assumed."

"Pampered?" Pablo choked. "You thought *he* was pampered?"

"You know the celebrity type." Macy rolled her eyes when Duke looked over at her. "Always having someone doing things for them."

He touched his heart and sank bank into the cushions of the couch. "*Athle-tante* is what you called it, right?"

Macy shrugged and hid her smile.

"So what happened to your usual helpers?" Mario

asked, perching himself on an arm of the couch just above Monique.

"They got tickets and a hotel for the Miami game."

"*The* Miami game?" Pablo leaned closer, scratching at his chin. He cut his best friend a glare. "You don't say?"

Duke shot his friend a glowering smile. Pablo knew about the tickets, as well as the hotel. Before seeing Macy, Duke had planned on taking Pablo down for the game. Of course everything else fell into place for him with Andy and Spencer. Now was not the time for a confession, but eventually he'd tell Macy the truth. It was best to change the subject. He looked up at Mario and guessed that would be a great way to start. "So what line of work are you in, Mario?"

"Landscaping." Mario whipped out a business card from the small square pocket of his tank top. "Let me know if you need any help."

"God, Mario," Monique groaned, "only you would try to make connections at a birthday party."

Mario blew a kiss at Monique. Duke took the card and looked at it briefly before slipping it into the back pocket of his jeans. "Are you ready for work, Mo?"

"A little bit. I'm enjoying the time I have with Lucia."

The longer he was covering her position, the more time he got to spend with Macy. The room filled with the rest of their guests. Francisco Cuomo, Macy's paternal grandfather, came over for a little while, just long enough to share a few stories of Macy's childhood and her bad temper. As soon as he left, Macy begged Duke to forget everything her grandfather said and just remember that she'd learned to overcome her anger through her mother's side of the family.

Duke got a chance to meet the younger Mario, MJ, when he and Wellinson, Pablo's son, came inside to see how much longer the food was going to take. When the kids opened the door, Duke's stomach growled at the delicious smell of the grill going. After a while the men, Duke included, went outside to check on the grill. Apparently Mario was manning it and seemed to be doing a good job.

Typically when Duke was gathered in the center of a male conversation, everyone wanted to know about his history with the Yankees. Since Duke's passion was baseball, he didn't mind it too much. Growing up, he'd always felt he was best at the sport. Before he hit eighteen, the pros were already calling. Instead of jumping into the major leagues, Duke opted to get an education first. He missed the days of living in the DR and being able to play all the time, all year long. When he became a sports reporter, he was still connected to the game, even though he covered all sports from baseball to golf to football. Most of his friends who weren't in the business were always curious about his ability to get tickets for games, whether for the Super Bowl, the World Series, or even big-time college football, like the one last night in Miami.

Pablo was staring at his best friend when Mario brought up the game this weekend. "You aren't fooling anyone," Pablo said once Mario left to bring in some cooked meat. "I know you got rid of Spencer and Andy."

Coyly, Duke smiled and took a long gulp of his beer.

The sun was shining brightly. He was glad he'd worn a T-shirt and jeans, but wished slightly to have worn some shorts as Pablo had.

Macy had a huge backyard. Pablo's kids and other children were playing a game of tag, screaming and running around like crazy. He remembered those days when he and Pablo used to run around like that. There wasn't much he and Pablo didn't share. "I'm pleading the fifth."

"Because you're guilty."

"Of being infatuated," Duke admitted.

"So what is the deal?" his friend asked. "You've obviously found your way in with her. Now what do you plan on doing with it?"

Duke leaned against the brick wall near the grill. "I'm not sure. She strikes me as hesitant about going any further with me, other than a few kisses here and there."

Pablo choked on his beer. "You kissed her?"

"I'm not going to kiss and tell."

"But you will with me." Pablo grinned and took another sip to clear his throat. "I told you Macy is special. Don't pull any stunts with her."

He didn't have to be told that Macy was special. "I know that. And I'm fine with the way things are right now. I really enjoy just being able to spend time with her. She's unlike anyone I've ever met."

"And speaking of people you've met, Kristina called the station looking for you. She's been getting a bit testy with my secretary, too."

Duke guessed Kristina had given up on contacting him by phone after he let her daily calls go straight to voice mail. Daily turned into weekly. After a few weeks of this, Duke just blocked her number and sent her emails straight to the trash. He half expected Kristina to give up on contacting him, but being the reporter that she was, she wasn't going to let go until they spoke. But he had no desire to speak to her and he had no desire to think of her right now, now that he was finally enjoying himself. He made a mental note to eventually call her back. Pablo's secretary, Desiree, didn't deserve harsh treatment from Kristina. But he didn't want to think about that today, either.

Blatantly changing the subject, Duke sighed. "So the kids are doing great with the new baby?"

"Just fine. As a matter of fact, Lucia will be christened the week after New Year's. I know your deal with Orsini says you have to return New Year's Day to renegotiate with MET. Do you think you can make it back?"

That just put things into perspective for Duke. He knew he was going to have to leave. The main reason Macy didn't want to get too involved with him was because she thought he was going to have to leave. His date to renew his contract with the MET Network was looming. If he chose not to return to the news desk in DC, his agent might find a station in Florida for him. After being away for so long Duke had a hard time strumming up the desire to return after that lifestyle. He had plenty of money to stay in Tallahassee for a while, whether it was at WKSS or not. He had no reason to get back. "I might just not leave."

Judging from the surprised look on Pablo's face, the news was unexpected. "Are you serious?"

Casually, Duke tossed his head back to laugh, with full intent to spy on Macy through the sliding glass door. She was facing him, but seated on the coffee table, playing with the baby and talking to Monique. Occasionally she would look up, tuck her hair behind her ear and smile in his direction. Every fiber of his being was on fire. He doubted he'd have a moment alone with her right now, but all he wanted to do was hold her in his arms and kiss her again. He appreciated how she made sure at her own birthday party that everyone was welcomed into her home, how she treated them like family. It was something his mother used to do—very warm and inviting.

"I'm serious as a heart attack."

"This is great for the station! I can rearrange things. Mo, of course, wants to come back, but I can figure out where to put you in the station. With your work in DC, you could handle the politics in Tallahassee with ease."

Before Duke could tell Pablo to hold off on etching his name onto an office door, Wellinson came over with MJ. Wellie gave Duke a high five. The boy was getting tall for eight years old. Wellie was his partner in crime. Back when he was a baby, Duke used to take him to the park, and the boy had become a babe magnet, not that Duke needed it.

Now he stood there right beside Duke, both of them waiting for Pablo to look the other way. They had their chance when Pablo lifted the grill to flip a few burgers. Duke slipped Wellie a ten-dollar bill. It had been his tradition to slip the kids some money on the side.

"Wellie says you played baseball," MJ said, tugging

at the hem of Duke's shirt. "He said you were a short-stop like me."

"That's right, I was," Duke answered with a grin. Now was his chance to win over the boy for whom he'd spoiled Christmas. "Do you want to play a bit?"

Enthusiastically MJ nodded his dark head. "Can we?"

"Can we what?" the boy's father asked, opening the screen door with a tray full of raw meat.

"Play baseball," Wellie and MJ chorused.

"Sure, why not? We have a few minutes before the food is all done," Mario said. "I call Duke's team!"

The sun had begun to set by the time the game was over. The food had been ready for a while, and tables covered in red-and-white checkered cloths were set up out back to accommodate all the guests who had arrived. Hamburgers, ribs, fish, potato salad—everything imaginable at a summer picnic was available for this late-November birthday feast. The pièce de résistance was the three-foot-tall birthday cake with candles on top. He stood next to Macy as she pulled her hair back and blew out the candles. Her face was bright red with embarrassment as everyone sang "Happy Birthday" to her. He liked that about her.

After several pieces of the chocolate cake, Duke found himself full. He collapsed in a cushiony lounge chair in the corner of the porch. Monique and Pablo had to leave to get the kids home and in bed for school in the morning. A few other neighbors and friends left, as well. MJ sat at Duke's side, still going on about the things he'd learned. Macy had gone up front to say goodbye to the rest of her guests.

"Thanks for teaching me all that stuff today," MJ said.

"Oh, no problem—anything for you." And it was the truth. Duke easily took a shining to the boy.

"Are you being extra nice because you outed Santa?"

"W-what?" The question obviously caught him off guard. Duke jumped to his feet.

No one told him that MJ was precocious. He sat there, grinning devilishly. "It's okay. My mom freaked out about it, but I already knew Santa wasn't real. I've known since I was a kid."

"You did?" Unfamiliar with this territory, Duke scratched the back of his head. "But your mom…"

"She loves Santa. I've just been pretending to believe in him, but I already know she's the one who puts the presents under the tree."

Duke cleared his throat. *Where is Macy?* Or where was Mario, for that matter? "Well, you see…"

"It's okay—" MJ stood up and patted Duke on the arm "—I'm going to tell my mom next year I know." Then he held out his little hand. "Let's just keep that our little secret."

Not knowing what else to say or do to that, Duke extended his hand and shook MJ's. He wouldn't say anything to Macy yet about him knowing about Christmas. Who knew? MJ might get a big surprise this year.

"Now that looks like a nice picture," Mario said, coming out the back sliding glass door. "MJ, I'm about to go. Walk me out?"

"Sure." MJ turned his head up at Duke and winked. "Thanks again."

Mario stepped forward and also extended his hand, just as his son had a few minutes ago. "Duke, it was a pleasure to meet you and play a game of baseball."

There was still the strong pressure in Mario's hand—dominance. Duke squeezed back hard, as well. "No problem. You should have been in the pros. You certainly have the arm for it."

Letting go of his hand, Mario flexed his throwing arm. "Sure, I had the arm for it, not the discipline. But thanks for the compliment. And I'll see you at the Ugly Sweater Party, right?"

"The what?" Duke leaned in closer, just in case he hadn't heard correctly.

Mario chuckled. "Ask Macy about it."

"Ask Macy what?" Macy asked, appearing in the doorway. Their eyes met and Duke felt his heart flutter and sink to the pit of his stomach with excitement. It had been a while since he felt this kind of exhilaration from eye contact with a woman. He liked the way she lowered her lashes and blushed. She tucked a strand of hair behind her ear as if to help distract herself. "The Ugly Christmas Sweater Party," MJ answered for everyone. "You have to wear the ugliest sweater you own, and if yours is the ugliest, then you win."

"Duke, you don't seriously want to go to that, do you?" It was the first time all evening Gia had said a complete sentence in front of him. She still had her phone in her hands, but her friends were gone. She'd changed into a pair of baggy sweats and her face was devoid of any makeup, reminding him even more of her mother. "Mom!" Gia shrieked with widened eyes. "You can't let Duke embarrass himself like that! It's one thing if Dad does it, but one bad picture could ruin his career!"

"Hey, I'm just finding out about this." Macy leaned against the door frame, her arms folded delicately across her chest. "Mario, would you go home and quit causing trouble around here?"

"Okay, okay. Kids, walk me out."

And finally, they were alone.

Duke breathed a sigh of relief. He had enjoyed spending time with everyone, but it was the first time in three straight days that he hadn't spent the whole day with her alone. The percussion-filled beat of a Milly Quezada song filtered through the speakers.

"Ah, the Queen of Merengue," he said with a smile. "What do you know about this?"

Macy shrugged. "I know a little somethin'."

"I've wanted to do this with you all day." He walked to her and extended his hand.

She took his hand and allowed him to pull her against his body. To the beat of the music, he moved their bodies as one in a slow dance. "You know how to merengue?"

"I'm Dominican," Duke responded simply.

Macy grinned and rolled her eyes. "I'm not even going to question that."

They danced for a few minutes. He could feel her heart beating and was sure she could hear his heart as she laid her head on his chest. Each step she took, right to left or back and forth, just sent images in his mind of how good things really could be between them. He meant what he said when he told Pablo that he wouldn't mind staying here. Something about Macy made him feel at home. The music stopped, but they stood together in the growing moonlight.

Macy looked up at him, batting her lashes. "My kids loved you. You even got Gia to speak with her mouth and not her Twitter."

"I loved your kids. They're great, and you've done a wonderful job with them."

"Thanks."

"Have you opened your present?"

When she shook her head no, her hair released the intoxicating scent of coconut. "I was waiting until everyone went home."

"You should open it now."

"I can't with you watching."

"I'll wait out here and you let me know if it's okay."

In protest, Macy wrapped her arms around his shoulders and molded her body against his. It killed him to peel her off, but he did and turned her around by her bare shoulders. "I'll be out here waiting."

Grudgingly, she turned and disappeared inside. Duke went back to the lounge chair and stretched his long legs. He thought about how he really could get used to these warm Tallahassee nights during the holidays. This time last year, he was wearing a wool coat, gloves and a scarf just to keep warm. He'd spent the holidays reporting. And last year he'd made a promise that he was going to get back home to Mao for the holidays. If he wasn't working.

Sure, he was working somewhat this season, but it was different. He was with Macy. His thoughts got lost in all the things he wanted to do with her. Time passed into minutes. After a while he realized Macy hadn't come back out. He wondered if she'd fallen asleep. Was he supposed to have let himself out? Curious, he got up from his lounge chair with a moan and went to the door; it was slightly open. He found Macy curled up on the end of the couch staring at the television, crying.

Panic surged through his veins. Her eyes were bloodshot red, and her nose matched. "Did I do something wrong? What is it?"

Sniffling, Macy untucked her legs from her position in the couch. She clicked off the remote control and slowly walked toward him. "I can't believe…"

"Was it wrong?" Duke smacked himself upside the head. "That was so stupid of me. I'm so sorry I didn't…"

She cut him off, throwing herself at him, wrapping her arms tightly around his neck, bringing him down to her level. Her tongue swooped into his mouth, capturing his tongue, claiming his mouth. Her hands clasped the sides of his face. His libido went into overdrive as she allowed him to bring her back down to the couch.

He still didn't have a clear idea why she was crying, but his body could only react to her soft lips against his. Her long dress was gathered around her thighs. Duke kissed her neck and then her shoulders. He peeled back the top of her dress for just a peek at one perfectly pink pert nipple. He ducked his head down for one quick taste. She gasped beneath his touch, and her fingers dug into his shoulders.

The front door slammed shut, and like two naughty teenagers, Duke and Macy scrambled to sit up. He helped her pull the top of her dress up and adjust her hair back over her shoulder. Her eyes were still glassy as she giggled and pulled his shirt down. He hadn't even realized she'd managed to pull it up so much.

"Hey, Mom!" Gia said, coming down the hall. She leaned over the ledge and looked at them.

"Are you crying?" MJ asked.

With a choked sob, Macy began to cry again. Duke cursed inwardly. Now the kids were going to think he was some sort of creep.

"They're happy tears," she reassured them.

"I think I upset your mom with her birthday present," Duke tried to explain. The kids came down the hall and into the living room. Gia sat on the couch and pulled MJ into her lap.

"What happened?" she asked.

"He just gave me a wonderful present that I never thought I'd ever get the chance to see."

"What did he give you?" MJ asked.

"My parents…" Macy sniffed. "It was a video of the Macy's Thanksgiving Day parade, the day I was born."

Duke eased back into the cushions of the couch with satisfaction. Finding the tape and getting it shipped here had been totally worth the effort, just to see the look of surprise and appreciation on Macy's face. His gesture to bring her a piece of her past opened up the doors for a brighter future for the two of them.

Chapter 6

With the Thanksgiving holiday behind them, the Christmas spirit began to spread to everyone in town. Thanks to Duke's help, Macy completed one of her most successful weekends yet. He'd turned out to be more reliable than expected. What she did not expect was her overflow of emotion for him. This celebrity crush was manifesting into something else, and Macy had no idea what to do with it. Since laying eyes on him in person, he'd had such a profound effect on every aspect of her life, and it was hard accepting he would be gone after the New Year.

Every day after he did the morning show, Duke would show up at Winter Paradise, just as promised. He worked diligently, helping her get all her homes done ahead of schedule. At the office, he bonded with Andy and Spencer while loading and unloading the shed. For Serena, he would call up his single friends and talk her up. If she ever made it to New York City or DC, she was going to have a busy time.

And then there were the evenings when Duke would insist on driving her home, and of course Gia and MJ would beg him to stay for dinner. When he talked about going out and finding a Christmas tree to chop down, the kids invited themselves to tag along, which led to an impromptu road trip after school. Of course, upon returning home, they had to show him the proper way to decorate a tree. Macy and the children always decorated their trees alone. But having Duke in the house with them seemed natural.

In just a short amount of time, Duke had become an intricate part of her life. And now Macy had plenty of time to work on his home. The Wainwrights ended up deciding not to go with Macy's company, which was fine with her. The positive side of not working with the Wainwrights meant it now gave her more time to work on Duke's place. After receiving written permission from the owners of the house Duke rented, Macy set forth a plan to work on the decorations.

Taking her eyes off her work for a second, Macy briefly looked up and spied Duke straddling the other end of the black shingles on the roof with the hammer in one hand, a nail in the other and an extra nail in his mouth. His triceps glistened in the sunlight. Sweat trickled from his brow, and he'd never looked sexier. The man concentrated on his task at hand, and maybe more so because they were finally able to work on his house, albeit in the evening. Of course he would have to have a two-story colonial-style home. It was pretty; Macy had seen the prestigious neighborhood when she searched for a home for her family. No matter how successful her business was, this neighborhood was still nowhere near her price range.

They'd spent the earlier part of their afternoon wrapping lights around the four pillars on his front porch. With the shutters being black, Macy thought it would be best just to light candles and hang wreaths on the four large windows on the bottom floor and hang more from the ones on the second floor. They were working on framing the top of the house with white lights, and more or less eye-flirting with a few stolen glances, her batting her lashes at him, and sending a few smiles back and forth after getting caught checking out one another.

And she had to give the man credit where credit was due; he certainly did know how to fill out a pair of jeans. The dark blue Yankees shirt he wore wasn't too bad, either. It fit across his broad chest like a second skin. She could almost feel those strong arms around her now. But Duke had been nothing but a gentleman. And as much as she hated to admit it, she was waiting for him to kiss her again. The thought of making out with him on her couch caused such a fire in her belly that she barely needed a jacket for the cooling weather.

"Are you watching me?" Duke asked with the nail still between his lips.

"I'm just making sure you're hitting the nail on the head." Macy recovered her composure. "I would hate for you to knock a hole in your roof. It might not rain right now, but the summers are notorious for afternoon showers."

"Lucky for me I won't have this house in the summer." Duke chuckled. He swung his hammer once and then extracted the other nail. Carefully he scooted closer toward Macy with the other string of lights following him.

The comment left a sour note in Macy's ears, reminding her once again he would be leaving. Was there really a point in getting involved with him? Monique had highly encouraged it after their talk last Sunday at her birthday. She'd known Duke since college and said she hadn't ever seen the glow he'd been sporting since getting involved with her. Serena had confirmed the same thing about Macy when they were alone at work together. Both women felt an affair was exactly what was needed. But Macy wasn't sure she was that kind of girl.

Duke was a heartthrob in the outside world. He was used to fast living, fast cars and fast women. And he was going back to that world. Macy's everyday life as a working soccer mom didn't fit in with that. Right now, he was miles away from it. Though a lot of people were mad at Duke for outing Santa just before Thanksgiving, he still had a huge following. A few people in town had stopped them when they were out together. There were the occasional homeowners who conveniently stayed home once they heard Duke Rodriguez was helping her out for the chance to meet him. She'd seen the photos in the tabloids of Duke spotted at celebrity and political events and had no idea how she would handle seeing him in person at a red carpet event with women throwing themselves at him.

She didn't think she could have a brief affair. No matter how good it physically would have felt, she didn't think she could survive the heartache once it ended. She knew she would get too attached to him, and recovering from a broken heart was not on her list of things to do.

Inhaling deeply, Macy tried to think about how she was going to handle things. She didn't want to fall in love with a man like Duke Rodriguez. A Mariah Carey tune about what she wanted for Christmas blasted from her truck's radio.

BAM!

Torn from her thoughts, Macy watched Duke hammer. "Are you following the pencil pattern I drew?"

"Yes, Miss Macy," he mocked.

Macy shrugged her shoulders, hit her nail on the head and scooted closer as well, making sure her next nail hung exactly where it was supposed to. "Did being a smart-ass get you were you are today?"

The hammer in his hand stopped in midair. He looked up and gave her a devil-may-care grin. Macy told herself she wasn't the devil and she didn't care. So what if his mouth looked so inviting? So what if he had dimples so deep, you could swim in them? Those chocolate-brown eyes weren't going to work on her. "Do you mean did my smart ass get me on top of the roof with a beautiful woman who knows how to work a hammer?"

Tugging a stray hair behind her ear to keep from blushing, Macy shook her head. "I stand corrected. It must have been flattery."

Bam. One hit on the head again and the nail sank into his roof. He moved closer to the center.

Not bad, she mused at his work. Macy tapped her nail twice and then hit it all the way in. She moved closer.

Another amused laugh filled the air as Duke reached for another nail out of his back pocket. He slipped one out and a second one behind his ear. "I didn't get here on just flattery and sarcasm," Duke said. "I worked very hard to get where I am, you know."

"Yes, from New York to DC." Macy hummed and hammered.

"Well, there were a lot of small towns along the road."

"Which is better?"

"Small towns or big?" Duke held his hammer in mid-air again and pondered that thought. His eyes glanced skyward for a moment before settling on hers. "There's good in both, I guess."

"Where has your favorite been?" She hammered and moved closer.

Duke looked down and hit the nail, scooted closer and took out two more nails. "Here."

"Here?" Macy half laughed. "I find that hard to believe."

Repeating his task, Duke moved closer. "Why? You're here."

"I was raised here," Macy said, as if that made a difference.

"But you didn't leave." He hammered and slid again. Her heart slammed against her rib cage with each inch he came toward her. "Did you think about leaving?"

Had she thought about leaving? She wanted to laugh, but it was too tragic that she couldn't. For as long as Macy could remember, her grandparents had raised her. But Tallahassee was also her parents' home, and the idea of leaving made her feel as if she was betraying their memory. "I've thought about it. But it was never the right time."

"Kids?" Duke nodded with understanding. The closer he got, the more Macy found herself studying his face. His cheekbones were high and his jawline squarely chiseled. There was a bit of a five-o'clock shadow on his face, which only made him look dangerous. She guessed a man who was into sports and a reporter wouldn't have seen the reason to stay in one place.

"Sure, kids kept me here. I mean—" she half shrugged "—there was school, and then Mario was here, and my grandparents. There were lots of reasons to stay here. I like the peace and quiet. I saw what living in the limelight did to my parents as famous reporters, and when they died, I even experienced it." Macy exhaled a sad sigh at Duke's quizzically raised brows. "A couple of reporters bombarded my grandparents' door when they died, shoving cameras in our faces asking how we felt about their deaths. I barely had time to process anything, and there they were. I don't see how you deal with it."

"I don't miss it," Duke admitted. "I've gotten so used to the little amount of fans I have here."

Macy offered a half smile before fiddling with a bulb on the string of lights. If Duke hadn't been in the limelight, she never would have developed a celebrity crush.

Of course, now she realized his TV and real lives were totally different. She much preferred the man before her.

"Do you at least travel, as in a vacation?" he asked, breaking her train of thought. In the distance, a train's horn blew and bells rang, indicating its arrival.

Macy shook her head no. For no reason at all, she did not travel. Thanks to the income she earned over the holidays, she had nothing to do during the spring and summer but plan for the next holiday.

"You ought to. I like Tallahassee, but I can admit that I miss seeing the seasons change. You know, right about now it would be snowing in New York City."

"I've never seen snow," Macy replied. She was used to the look on everyone's faces when she disclosed that information.

Duke's eyes bugged out. "Really? Your re-creations of snowy scenes are impeccable."

"It's a snowman." She gave a shrug and looked down at the ground.

"How could you not have seen snow?"

"Well, with my folks working, they came down here when they could for the holidays. I'd go up there for the summers."

"You've done such a fantastic job with your imagination, then." Duke nodded his head down toward his front lawn.

His yard was filled with a snowy Christmas scene that came straight out of a Norman Rockwell painting. Fake snow was sprinkled on the ground of Duke's spacious front yard. He didn't have many trees, which made some decorating easy. It was only hard because she had to use what leftover statues she had in storage. Coming up from the driveway, she created a real bridge that looked wooden from afar but was made of a simple hard plastic. Snow covered the railings.

On one side of the bridge, Macy had carefully put statues of fawns playing. Underneath the bridge, she created a small pond. She hid the extension cord underneath the snow and plugged it in around back. On the other side of the bridge was a snowman equipped with a fake carrot that looked real enough to eat. For good measure, she stuck coal from her grill down the front of the middle ball to represent a shirt.

"It's a great snowman. It looks like one I built my first time seeing snow." Duke hammered again and then moved closer. He chuckled to himself and shook his head. "My first snow, I sent my sisters a bag of it."

"Didn't it melt?"

"Yeah, even with express mail."

Macy leaned back and laughed, imagining what it might have been like to get that in the mail. Duke was really turning into someone she couldn't have imagined. He liked his family, he was kind and he was, in his own way, humble. He wasn't afraid of hard work or taking orders.

"Have you brought them here to see snow?"

Smiling, Duke slowly nodded his head. "I've brought my sisters here. My parents haven't been."

"Ever?"

"No. You see, where I'm from, the Christmas countdown starts in October, and my folks are really busy."

"I told you I'm the type of person who gets excited

about the Christmas displays before Halloween," Macy said, leaning in, listening.

Duke nodded. "I noticed that. There's something about being home and smelling your mother's and aunts' cooking. Bosses hand out double *sueldo*..."

"Bonuses?"

With a wink, Duke smiled. "Not just any bonus. It's pretty much what you make in a month. It helps spread cheer for families that might not have enough to spend on their kids. On Noche Buena—Christmas Eve—we go to a special mass called La Misa del Gallo."

As he filled her with stories of back home, there was a certain sadness in Duke's voice that Macy couldn't miss. "You miss them, don't you?"

"I do, I miss my city. This sunset reminds me of it."

"Oh yeah? *Mao*. Did I say that right?"

"You did. But it was also called Ciudad de los Bellos Atardeceres."

She looked at him with one eyebrow raised for translation.

"The City of the Beautiful Sunsets. But right now, I'm beginning think it's the company you keep that makes someplace spectacularly beautiful."

Her heart lurched in her rib cage. She cleared her throat and tucked a nonexistent strand of hair behind her hear. "Maybe you should go back soon."

"I will one day. Maybe next year I'll go."

Again, Macy was reminded that Duke's being here was just temporary. She was going to miss him when he was gone.

"You didn't ask me why I like it here the best."

"Okay," Macy said slowly, uncomfortably. A part of her wanted to move away, but if she moved too quickly she would fall. She looked to her left, but the late-afternoon sun was setting earlier, leaving a beautiful orange glow that blinded her. Trees hugged Duke's backyard, and from this angle there was nothing but dense darkness.

Duke placed a hand on the roof, on either side of her hips. His eyes wide, he touched his forehead to hers. "Because if I hadn't come here, I wouldn't have met you."

"If you hadn't outed Santa…" she started to remind him, but then forgot all that she was going to say when his lips reached out and brushed hers. He pulled his head back to see if she was okay with it. Macy felt such a shock of pleasure that she smiled. She actually smiled at him.

He leaned in closer, turned his head to the right and closed his eyes. His upper body held his weight as he deepened the kiss. Their tongues touched with a zap of electricity. He must have felt it, too, because he pulled away for a second, just a second, and she felt him smile against her mouth. Macy wanted to lean closer, but that was too bold, and besides, she could fall.

Duke's hands touched her thighs, his thumbs on her inner thigh while his fingers spread across the thickness of her legs. Slowly they moved to the curve of her waist. As their tongues danced, his hands were on her back, and he pulled her closer to his chest. For a quick moment, Macy felt herself panic. This wasn't safe. This was dangerous. She couldn't breathe at first, and then she could feel his arms crossing over, and his fingertips held on to her shoulders.

Finally, she breathed.

She recalled one time when her *nonna* came home from the hospital with a small oxygen tank. Macy had wanted to see what it was like. Maybe now was not the time to recall that memory, but the thrill of the risk felt somewhat the same. Macy was so scared that she would get caught, but at the same time she could breathe with such clarity. Her lungs were clear; her mind was clear. She felt as if she were walking on a cloud.

"If I hadn't outed Santa," Duke finished for her, "I probably wouldn't have been able to kiss you."

Just then the phone in her back pocket rang. Macy looked at the number, frowned and answered it. She watched Duke's face as he watched hers, trying to read what was wrong. She hung up the phone after a few *okay*s and *uh-huh*s.

"Is everything okay?"

She half smiled. "It was just a reminder of why this—" she wiggled her hands back and forth between them "—is an impossible situation. My life is too complicated right now for a relationship."

Disappointed at her own admission, Macy pushed away, but Duke held on to her hand.

"What is it?"

"It's just one of those days. Gia's at school, and she had to stay late because her media teacher needed help while he was doing something else. Mario was supposed to pick her up, but he got caught up with MJ…"

She growled with frustration. "I'm sorry, but this is just typical of Mario. He's so irresponsible!"

Duke cupped her face and gently made her look at him. "So, okay, she needs a ride? Let's go get her."

"It's not just that, Duke." Macy felt herself melting looking into those eyes of his. "It's a ride today, a dozen cookies tomorrow. Someone is sick and puking in the future… My life is unpredictable, Duke, and your time here is short."

He dipped his head down, capturing her lips with his. Gently, his mouth coaxed hers open and his tongue slid across her lips, breathing life into her once again. "So let's go get Gia. I can help with cookies tomorrow, but hopefully no one will be puking later."

"You really didn't have to come with me," Macy was saying with her hand on the passenger's side of her truck. They were pulled up in front of the local high school. Duke had seen Macy angry before and was glad this time that he wasn't on the receiving end of it. If he'd had any questions about her relationship with Mario, it was all answered by the way she went off on him on the ride over. Apparently, Mario was supposed to pick up Gia after school, but got caught up at MJ's karate class. And that had been one of the basic complaints Macy had about him. Duke liked the guy, but even without being a parent himself, he knew you had to learn how to multitask. Apparently, things like today happened more often than not.

Duke released his seat belt and rushed out his door

to help Macy out, even though she had one leg on the ground. "You know I didn't mind. It's quite domestic."

He wiggled his eyebrows at her and ignored the fact that she rolled her eyes at him.

"If you like being domestic, I'll give you my grocery list." She slightly laughed. "I'll be right back here," Macy called over her shoulder as she entered the building. "Try to stay out of trouble."

Trouble. Duke snorted outwardly and leaned against the passenger-side door. He looked all around him. There were a few cars left in the pickup parking lot of the high school. When he was younger, there had been no one to pick him up, so he and his siblings had to walk. There were no buses, but their mother made sure each and every single one of them knew the importance of going to school. Duke had had coaches to keep him steady. If he didn't go to school, he wouldn't play.

In the distance, Duke thought he heard the familiar sound of a bat cracking against a ball. He'd know that sound anywhere. As if on autopilot, he headed toward the direction the sound came from. Off to the left of the building, he spied a baseball diamond. His pulse quickened, as it did every time he saw a field. His hands itched to throw a ball or swing a bat. A group of kids dressed in what Duke assumed were the school colors of blue and white were tossing around the ball. There was someone on the sidelines with a clipboard. The man didn't look tall enough, or nearly muscular enough, to have ever played ball before. Duke hadn't realized he was chuckling until the man looked up, waved and started walking over toward him.

"You're Duke Rodriguez!" the man stated.

"I am," Duke confirmed slowly as he extended his hand. "I didn't mean to interrupt your practice."

"Bah!" the man grunted with a flick of his wrist. Behind him the other members of the team were coming up the hill. "You weren't interrupting much. We're down a coach, as you may have heard. Oh my God, of course you heard. You commented on it on the news the other week when, you know…" The smaller man elbowed Duke in the ribs and with his other hand, covered his mouth and whispered, "When you outed Santa."

Here we go again, Duke sighed inwardly. "Yeah." He scratched at the back of his head. "I'm sorry about that, Coach."

"Don't be. I thought it was a hoot. Oh, where are my manners? I'm not the coach here. I'm the media teacher, Bob Nogowski. I'm just filling in until we can find a more suitable coach. Uh-oh, here they come." Bob nodded toward the boys coming up the hill.

The boys, all fifteen of them, all seemed to be over six feet fall, and each and every one of them spoke at once, introducing themselves and shoving their hands in front of Duke to shake. He did his best to keep up with the names. Out the corner of his eye, he spied Macy with Gia walking toward the car. He hoped he didn't embarrass Gia.

His attention was diverted momentarily as the kids asked questions like lightning. It amazed Duke that these kids could recall his batting average back in the day. They had to have been in elementary school when he had that old life. It also amazed him that he'd already been reporting the news for a few years now, and it dawned on him that everyone, besides Macy, always referred to his days as an athlete.

Within the crowd of questions, Duke heard someone clear her throat. He looked up and saw Macy standing behind him. Her arms were folded, but she had an amused crooked smile and one eyebrow raised. "You are such an athle-tante!" she teased.

One person who wasn't smiling was Gia. She looked more mortified than when he'd first met her. The last thing he wanted to do was upset her. Perhaps these were her friends and he was invading her privacy or something.

"Sorry, hon, I heard the swing of the bat and the rest was history. Hey, Gia, sorry if I kept you waiting."

"Gia, your mom's dating Duke Rodriguez?" one of the kids said to her.

"Uh, well…" Gia fumbled to find the words. She looked down and around, then toward her mother for help.

"We're very good friends," Macy supplied.

"Cool."

Duke wanted to say they were more than just friends, but he was a bit preoccupied watching Gia and another boy. Obviously, the two awkward teenagers wanted to talk to each other. The boy shuffled his feet in the dirt and twisted his body left and right in his letterman's jacket. Since he'd begun spending more time at the Cuomo household, Duke hadn't heard Gia mention anything about a boy. She talked about school, her media teacher and some of her girlfriends. But not a boy, not a boy in particular.

A sudden surge of protectiveness crept over him.

Duke remembered the boy's name was Jimmy and he was the only freshman on the varsity team. He was tall and lanky, but that was typical for a fourteen-year-old. He seemed like a good kid at first, but now that he was blushing the same shade of red as Gia, Duke wasn't too sure. Her eyes widened and her mouth dropped wide open.

Duke wrapped his arms around Macy's and Gia's shoulders. "Well, I've kept my two favorite ladies waiting. Guys, have a great season."

There was a bit of protest from the guys, including the temporary coach. Duke promised he'd try to come to one of their practice games before he left. Jimmy stepped over and tugged Gia's arm. She went with him to the side so they could speak privately. Duke kept a watchful eye out for them, just in case.

"Any time you want to come by," Bob said, shaking Duke's hand, "it would be perfectly fine with me. We could really use some pointers out here."

The team backed the coach up on his open offer. Duke started to shake his head no. He already had a job to do, and when he was done at the station he was rushing to spend time with Macy. "Well…"

"I'll be honest with you, I could use some help here," Bob said. "I'm the media pro. Ask Gia."

"You should," Macy encouraged him with a smile.

"I'll have to see what my schedule is like and I'll

have Gia let you know. She might not like me being around."

Jimmy and Gia rejoined them, some of the boys already pleading with Gia. Duke tucked Macy closer to his side as he said goodbye to everyone and walked off. When they got closer to the car and, more importantly, out of sight and earshot of the team, Gia did some odd skip move toward the car. She spun around at the locked door and faced them. Duke still had the keys and unlocked the door with them in his hand.

"Oh my God!" Gia squealed. "Jimmy actually knew my name! He's the first freshman to be on the varsity team! The *varsity team*! I am so excited! He wants to take me to the Christmas dance this next week! Can I, Mom? Can I? Oh my God! Thank you, thank you, thank you, Duke, for coming to pick me up!" With that, Gia pulled out her cell phone and began Tweeting as she entered the backseat.

Duke hadn't realized that Macy slipped her fingers into his as they walked toward the car until she squeezed his hand. "I think she's an even bigger fan of yours now."

"Oh yeah?" Duke beamed, aware of the crush Gia had had prior to meeting him. "How do you know?"

"She actually told you the news before you heard it on Twitter." Macy looked up and smiled. Seconds later, her phone was chirping, indicating a Tweet.

They stopped walking once they reached the back of the car. Duke turned her toward him and took both hands in his and smiled down at her. "That's progress, right?"

Her lashes batted against her cheeks as she looked down at his chest to contemplate his question. He liked the way her eyes turned a golden brown when the sun hit them just right. She was smiling, but the smile hadn't gone to her eyes. It reminded him of the first time he'd laid eyes on her and she wouldn't really look at him. Something was wrong.

"It's progress," she agreed.

"I hear a 'but' in there somewhere."

"The kids and I have really enjoyed spending time with you with this week. I just fear that they're going to get too close."

"What's wrong with that?"

"You still have a contract in DC." Macy looked down. "That means you're leaving once the New Year rolls around."

"Yes and no." Duke gave a long sigh. He hadn't shared his thoughts of staying on with the DC station with Macy. How crazy did it sound that he didn't want to leave Tallahassee? He enjoyed being able to sleep through the night and not have to get up at all kinds of hours to get a story. Macy and her children had helped him get ready for his upcoming party, and since last week, he absolutely looked forward to getting off work and finding out what they'd been up to all day. Family. He missed being a part of a family.

But what did he have to offer them? Macy wasn't interested in his fame. The children were over being starstruck. Without all that, was he still enough for them? When he returned to Mao last summer, his father thought Duke was crazy for taking a break from the career he'd worked so hard to build. His mother had stood up for Duke in her own way and reminded him that even with all the accolades he received and parties he attended, they did not mean as much without his own family. Duke half agreed. He did want a family, and one was waiting for him in DC with Kristina, but it wasn't the one he wanted. More and more, each day he saw himself with someone like Macy. He just didn't want to scare her off too soon. "Does that mean that we have to stop seeing each other when I leave?"

Her eyes lit up just as Gia's had a few moments ago. The idea obviously hadn't crossed her mind. "That can get expensive."

"Let me worry about that, okay?"

"Okay, Mr. Athle-tante."

He had plenty of money to travel back and forth if he wanted. He hadn't been a careless athlete. He'd helped out his folks as much as they would let him and then kept the rest of his signing money away in savings. Then of course there had been the money from his job at ESPN and now. "I've got that covered. I just want you to stop bringing up New Year's Eve being the end of things, because it doesn't have to be."

Macy stood up on her tiptoes, bringing her lips to his. "I like the sound of that. And I'll try not to bring up New Year's Eve."

Duke responded at first with a kiss, slow, sensual and meaningful. He pulled away and wrapped his arms tighter around her waist. "Well, that's the best Christmas present ever!"

Chapter 7

Mario's annual Ugly Christmas Sweater Party was in full swing by the time Macy and Duke arrived with the kids. His two-story house was filled with friends from work and friends from way back in the day. The kids made a plate from the buffet table and disappeared. Last year, Macy recalled, Mario recruited her for last-minute details. This year things went off without a hitch, which only made Macy happy because now she had plenty of time to spend with Duke. Macy shared a few pastries with Duke before he was pulled away by a group of guys for sports talk.

To keep up with the theme tonight, Macy wore a minidress decorated to look like a Christmas tree, garnished with tiny red, green and gold balls. She clinked every time she walked, and she hung out by the fireplace, occasionally stealing glances across the room and enjoying every butterfly flittering around her stomach. She twisted a strand of her flat-ironed hair around her forefinger. Gia had spent all evening on her hair and would have had a fit if she saw her twisting it. Letting it go, Macy inhaled deeply, agreeing with everything Serena yammered on about. Macy nodded in the direction where Duke was standing and talking to Mario and Pablo.

Serena had encouraged Macy to give in to her libido where Duke was concerned, but she had no idea how complicated her life was with Duke in the picture. In the afternoons when it was slow, Duke offered to pick up Gia from school after he helped the baseball team with drills. Some days, he would bring MJ with him to help chase balls. After practice and work, he would come by Macy's office, pick her up and take them all out to eat. In the evenings when homework was due, he would help out, whether it was Gia with her media class or MJ with his math, while Macy worked on dinner. When the kids went to bed, she and Duke would sit on the couch, kissing away like two teenagers until it became too uncomfortable for either one of them. Both had agreed not to do anything silly, like getting caught on the couch by Gia or MJ. And Duke's spending the night would seem to send the wrong message for the kids. So Duke and Macy were forced to handle their relationship like grown, mature adults. A lot of cold showers were taken on Macy's part.

Last night, Gia asked Duke to take her to the upcoming dance with Jimmy. Having a Ferrari could have had something to do with it. And it had been Gia who picked out the green cardigan Duke wore tonight, with a snow-man family down at the bottom; what looked like snow falling on the family was actually cotton balls sewn onto the garment. It fit. It fit well, Macy thought, look-ing at Duke's broad shoulders stretching the green twill.

In her eyes, Duke was the epitome of the perfect man. Besides having a sculpted body of a god, he knew how to make her feel like the only woman in the room—in the world, even, whenever he looked at her. Sure, he had a megawatt smile that dazzled her each time she looked at him and his kisses brought every fiber in her body to life. But it was beyond the hard body, seduc-tive dark eyes, or his chivalry. It was that and more that made Duke so desirable.

When they were together, he hung on to every word she said, listened to idle chatter from Gia and MJ. He was creative with the children, even when they bick-ered with each other, overdramatizing the issue they were fighting about, though the conflict usually ended with the kids defending each other. With MJ, Duke figured out how to distract him from being sad over Mario forgetting to take him to get a haircut. Duke talked MJ into going with him to the barber and they both came home with fresh cuts. According to MJ, the barber gave the boy a hot towel facial while he trimmed Duke's dark goatee. He was good with the children. He was good with her.

When she had mocked his hands weeks ago, she had no idea of the tenderness behind his fingers. The way he stroked her face when he kissed her goodbye, or the control he maintained when reaching over to massage her shoulders and feet after a long day. Every time he glanced at her with his deep brown eyes, he bored through another wall inside her. When he touched her with his large hands, every inch of her body wanted to melt. The past few nights, they had a few intimate moments on her couch. Macy could not believe how out of control she could get with him. Just the other night, she'd ripped off his shirt and almost begged him to make love to her on the couch downstairs, but he remained levelheaded. It wasn't as if he hadn't taken his shirt off when they worked during the day, but when the man stood hovered over her body on the couch at night, with candles set all around them, it was hard not to shake the feeling of his hard abs against her fingertips. But because she knew what he looked like without that sweater, it made the whole thing ridiculously funny at the same time. Macy inhaled deeply and focused on the man at hand.

It was a good thing Duke was so confident. He was good-natured through it all, teasing her and calling her a *celebutante* when someone would pull her to the side just to let her know they were voting for her homes in the decorating contest. He didn't seem to mind at all when her former client, Lawrence Hobbs, came over to wish her good luck on the drawing tonight when she was standing off to the side while Duke had gone to get them something to drink. When Duke arrived, Macy made the introductions and Lawrence was on his way. He wasn't bothered at all by the pilot. *It's nice to be in a mature relationship*, she mused to herself.

"Ugly sweater be damned," Serena said, holding her cup of eggnog in front of her mouth. No amount of slurping on the beverage could mask her grunted moan. "That man looks good."

"I will have to agree to that," Macy said, toasting her cup of apple cider in Duke's direction.

"Isn't it weird that Mario has a man crush on your boyfriend?" Monique asked, coming over to the two ladies. She wore a black sweaterdress with Santa on it that buttoned down the front. On the left side of the dress, Santa looked as if he was tiptoeing away, dragging his sack of toys behind him, but instead of toys spilling out of the open bag, it looked more like cotton padding, as if Monique stuffed her bra.

"I have two things to say." Macy looked at the outfit and laughed. "First, let me say that I hate you for getting your body back so quickly after having Lucia!"

Looking down at herself, Monique blushed. "Sorry, but I have been working double time to get things back in place before I show my face on high-definition television again."

"That's why I'm never having kids," Serena chimed in. "All that extra work to lose the weight? No thanks." She shook her head. Macy and Monique shared a look, knowing they had once both said the same thing before in their lifetimes.

"So what was the second thing you wanted to say?" Monique asked, ever the reporter. She hadn't forgotten how Macy had phrased her statement.

"Oh." Macy shrugged and took another look at Duke across the room. He looked at her at that exact moment and gave her a wink. The status of their relationship hadn't been publicly announced. She knew what they were when they were alone, but Macy wasn't sure if she wanted the world to know. What would happen when he went back to his celebrity lifestyle in DC and she had to watch his life pass her by in the tabloids from Tallahassee? "He's not my *boy*friend."

"Whatever! Man-friend, gentleman caller." Monique playfully pushed Macy's shoulder. "I hear down at the station that he's so eager to wrap up in the morning just so he can get over here to help you out."

"So?"

"So?" Monique stood there and gaped. "So as a reporter, you're only as good as your next story, and he hands off every bit of good news that comes across his desk."

That was something Macy wasn't aware of. She just assumed that because of Duke's high profile, there wasn't much investigative reporting he could do. "Oh, I didn't realize that."

"Did you also realize that Gia's dropped her crush on Duke?" Monique pressed on. "I haven't gotten a single Tweet about him and what he wore. Now it's all about some guy named Jimmy."

Macy had noticed she hadn't heard much else about Gia's love for Duke. Gia wasn't the first one anymore to turn on the television in the morning to catch Duke's broadcast while she got ready. Macy had figured that as a typical thirteen-year-old, she'd found someone else to crush on. "What do you think that means?"

"I think it means she's giving her mom permission to

steal her man," Serena interjected. "And I have stepped down from being the future Mrs. Rodriguez, as well."

"Oh, that's so generous of you," Monique said drolly.

Poking out her tongue, Serena leaned in closer to Macy. "And he'd be your boyfriend if you gave him some."

"Serena!" Macy blushed. "No."

"Why the hell not?" both girls blurted out. A group of Mario's guests looked at them as they walked by. The ladies regained their composure.

Monique leaned in closer and whispered, "Y'all haven't?"

Macy shook her head. "No, sorry to disappoint you guys."

"Again, I have to ask, why the hell not?" Monique laughed. "He might be my husband's best friend, but the man is gorgeous and totally into you!"

Leaning in, Serena whispered to Monique, not quietly enough though, "And you heard about the birthday present he got her, right?"

"No, what?"

"He gave her a copy of the tape of the Macy's Thanksgiving Day parade her parents were covering when her mother went into labor with her."

"Aw!" Monique covered her mouth, but not before Macy spotted her poking her bottom lip out. "He's your *angelito*!"

"My what?"

Shrugging, Monique dropped her hands to her side. "It's a Dominican tradition I've learned from Pablo. Each week, you receive a gift."

"Like a secret Santa."

"Something along those lines."

"So what are you going to give him in return?" Serena leered, wiggling her eyebrows up and down.

"When do you guys think I would have time for something like that? The kids do live with me."

"Do you want me to have them spend the night tonight with me?" Monique asked. "Maylen has been begging me to let her hang out with Gia since Gia gave her that makeover the last time she babysat them."

"We'll see." Macy shrugged. "We're in no rush."

"No rush? Don't you want to see what he's like in bed before he leaves?" Serena inquired.

As much as she wanted to find out, Macy still had standards to uphold. She rolled her eyes. "Not every relationship has to end up in sex, Serena."

"Well, all of mine have."

There hadn't been a serious or healthy relationship in Serena's life. She was young, though, no kids and in school. Macy shook her head and grinned. "And what kind of meaningful relationship are you in right now?"

Wincing, Serena pouted. "Ouch."

"Sorry." Macy tilted her head to the side and looked thoughtfully at her friends. "But we're in no rush because Duke said things didn't have to end after the New Year."

"Get out!" Monique's jaw dropped. "I didn't realize he was so serious about you."

"Apparently so." Macy beamed.

"And are you that serious about him?"

"I think I am."

"Well, if you sleep with him now, that can help you decide if you definitely are or aren't," Serena added. Macy made a mental note to not let Serena have another glass of eggnog.

Monique stood there, smiling. "I can't believe our two close friends are hitting it off so well. I think I'm going to cry!"

"Please don't," Macy quickly said as she reached out and stroked Mo's shoulder. "Let's see where things go before the waterworks come out."

Nodding, Monique sniffed back her tears. "Okay, I'll try not to."

"Or at least wait until they do the nasty," Serena mumbled.

What Macy didn't tell her friends was that tonight the kids were spending the night with Mario. When Duke took her home this evening, it would be the first time they were going to have a chance to be home alone. They'd been alone together before, but something about tonight was different. Duke had been a patient man. Despite each passionate kiss he gave her, she never felt pressured by him. It was nice to go out with a man who didn't expect more right away.

From across the room, Duke made eye contact with her. He stood as tall as Mario's Christmas tree, but he seemed broader than it. Her heart swelled at the sight of such a man. Duke broke the contact with a wink. He whispered something to Pablo and handed him his drink, then made his way across the room toward her. Macy felt her heart skip a beat as he approached.

Eartha Kitt's seductive croons of "Santa Baby" filtered through the air. Macy could think of one thing in particular she wanted. And by the end of the first verse, he was standing right in front of her.

"Care to dance?"

"Dance?" Macy managed to get out. Mario had moved all his furniture out, so that there was room for everyone. No one else was dancing. Before she could point out that fact, Duke pulled her by her wrists into the center of the room and held her against his hard body. Once again, his touch made her feel as if she was melting. Her knees went weak, but it didn't matter, Duke had her. His arms were wrapped around her waist, fingers resting at her backside. Against the fabric of his green sweater, his heart thumped through his chest. His square jawline twitched and his full lips broke into a smile.

Even with their height difference, Duke managed to crane his neck down to bring his lips close to hers. Macy's heart raced in anticipation of a kiss. For once, she was aware they weren't the only ones in the room. All eyes were on them and she claimed him, stretching her arms upward around his neck. Duke's thighs pressed against hers and they moved together as one. Everything was perfect. "Well, I guess that's a yes, then."

"Have I told you how beautiful you look this evening?"

She fit against his body comfortably, familiarly. "I think you may have said something about it when you picked me up."

"The statement still stands. I don't think I'm the only one who seems to think so, either." Duke nodded his head in the direction of Lawrence, who stood in the corner sipping his eggnog.

Macy cut her eyes back at Duke. "Well, thank you. Were you taking a poll?"

"No need. I'm Dominican. I can sense these things."

"Whatever," she said. "May I say how handsome you are?"

Duke grinned and nodded his head. "Thank you. You may."

"Well, all the ladies are discussing it, also."

"All of them?" he inquired with a raised eyebrow. "What about one in particular?"

"Which one were you concerned with?"

Chuckling, he grinned, exposing that devil-may-care dimple with his crooked smile. "I thought I was pretty sure I made myself clear as to which woman I was interested in on that first morning I came to work with you. But in case you need a reminder…"

Duke dipped his head and captured her lips in a sensual kiss. He tipped her chin up to meet his face. They swayed to the music, or so she thought. Macy felt as though she were floating on air. Somehow they danced like that until Nat King Cole's deep voice entered the room with "The Christmas Song."

"How are you enjoying your evening?" Duke asked.

Was it normal for a woman's body to be so turned on from a kiss? Macy's heart fluttered. "I think I'm enjoying it just fine. But then again, the night is still young."

"Oh yeah?" He pulled his head back to get a look at her. "What does that mean?"

She offered him a sly smile and shrugged in his

arms. "It means that the kids are spending the night with Mario."

"I think I heard him mention that. I know it sounds weird, but it was like he was giving me the go-ahead head nod."

Hiding her laugh, Macy pressed her head against Duke's broad chest. "That sounds about right."

"I have to admit that I was a bit jealous when I first met him."

"Really?" She craned her neck to look up at him. "Why?"

"Well, he is your ex-husband. You guys seemed very chummy."

She shook her head before he could say another word. "We're chummy now because we were friends before we got a divorce." Macy tried to pretend she did not hear sarcasm in his voice. "We have two kids together. I thought you would understand that in order to co-parent, we have to get along."

"Can I ask why you two split?"

She really didn't want to talk about Mario, especially when her body just wanted to be completely satisfied by Duke, but she felt she owed him that much of an explanation. "Let's just say that there were times that Mario just looked at me like we were buddies. And then one day this woman left a message at the house for him, letting him know that she wasn't pregnant after all."

"Ouch."

"It's okay." Macy shrugged. "At that point in our relationship, it was much more of a relief. I wasn't in love with him. I loved him and always will because he's one of my best friends, but I'm not in love with him."

"And you haven't dated anyone since because of him?"

"No, I haven't dated anyone because I was too busy running my own company."

"And now?"

"And now, I'm listening to my inner Grandma V's voice and taking time to stop and smell the roses."

"Who?"

"My Grandma Virginia," Macy explained. "My mother's mother."

She wanted to let Duke know at that moment that she was falling in love with him, but decided to save it for a more intimate setting. He looked down at her with half-closed lids. He was staring at her lips. And every time he did that, it made her blood pulsate.

"So, back to what I was saying," she brazenly said. "We'll have the house to ourselves."

Duke returned the sly smile. "Are you asking me to a sleepover?"

The image of them having a pillow fight on her bed filtered through her mind, though she highly doubted that kind of rolling around in the bed would happen. But the thought of what could happen made her stomach flip. She was ready. She was beyond ready. These cold showers she was taking every night were about to end.

"Maybe not the kind I used to have when I was a kid."

Duke cleared his throat and put a little distance between them. She'd gotten to know his body very well in the past few weeks. She knew he was as turned on and excited as she was, but his body reacted more physically when he was turned on. She thought it was cute how he would try to pull away. The first time she could recall him doing that was on Thanksgiving when they'd been interrupted by the phone call. She smiled, appreciated his being aroused by their kisses. At least she wasn't the only one.

"Be careful, Ms. Macy. I just might take you home right now."

A chill crept down her spine. Her cheeks heated in a blush. She wrapped her arms tighter around his shoulders and realized she could feel his heart beating. "And is there a problem with that?"

Dropping his hands from her waist, he took hold of her hand. "Let's get out of here."

Following his cue, Macy grinned and allowed Duke to maneuver her through the now-crowded floor full of dancers. The weather wasn't cold enough for a long coat, and even if it were, there was so much heat pumping through Macy's veins, she would have been fine outside. Duke stopped at the door. Macy looked up at him, feeling a slight disappointment. Had he changed his mind?

"Look." Duke pointed up toward the doorway. "Mistletoe. I think it's only proper that we practice the custom."

Before she could say anything, his lips had recaptured hers with the same kind of passion he'd shown a few minutes ago. Macy felt her blood pulsating. Knowing that the kids weren't going to be home all weekend long made her feel like a horny teenager. She giggled before deepening her kiss. "We should go. Now."

Duke reached for the door, but it was already opening. Macy was too busy grinning from ear to ear to pay attention. From across the room she could hear Serena whistle crassly at them sneaking off.

"Well, damn, Duke Rodriguez, if you aren't the hardest man to get a hold of."

Macy was still smiling and blushing when she turned to face who was at the door. The first thing she'd noticed was that Duke had dropped her hand, causing her to look at who was speaking.

"Kristina." Duke's warm voice had turned icy cold.

Kristina Barclay was as glamorous in person as she was on television. She was close to six feet tall with legs that went on for days. Obviously she didn't know it was an ugly sweater party; otherwise she wouldn't have poured herself into the black cashmere dress that stopped barely below her thighs and worn thigh-high black leather boots. She wore a black-and-white houndstooth coat to shield her from the dropping temperature. Macy bit the inside of her lip and studied the woman whom Duke had been so popularly linked to.

"Oh, you don't know how glad I am to find you here!" Kristina cooed. "I thought for a second that you might have actually flown home to that little village of yours. You always were talking about spending the holidays with your parents."

Macy had never been to Mao, but she took great offense at the way Kristina spoke of Duke's hometown. Knowing how much Duke cared about his family, she also didn't appreciate her dismissing Duke's love for them, either. How long had they known each other?

"Well, aren't you going to invite me in?"

"It's not my party, Kristina."

Unfortunately, Mario didn't catch the tension. "Kristina Barclay." He practically drooled as he pushed his way to the door. "Come in, come in!"

"Thank you," Kristina said, sauntering into the room. The music was still playing, but no one was dancing. Pablo had made his way across the room with Mario. "Pablo, haven't you been giving Duke my messages?"

"Now is not the time," Pablo said under his breath. Monique appeared at her husband's side.

"You knew she was coming?" Monique's question was more like a sentencing from a judge. Macy felt sorry for him because she knew Pablo was going to get an earful later.

"Now is exactly the perfect time." Her upper lip curled in a sneer as she looked at Pablo. "That senator from Tallahassee is stepping down. I would have thought you—" she turned and looked over her shoulder at Duke "—would have been all over it, seeing how you're in his hometown."

Pablo looked down at his phone. Macy looked around and noticed that everyone working for the station was checking their cell phone for the text messages. But not Duke.

Macy felt Duke tense again. "Not now, Kristina. Go away."

"I can't go away. The station has sent me down here

to this godforsaken town to cover the story. And Oscar wanted me to remind you that you're on loan here. Didn't you read the fine print?"

Duke spoke through clenched teeth. "I was rather preoccupied when I left."

"Well, your contract here is null and void with the station if there is a story. And—" she slipped off her coat, which Mario eagerly caught "—obviously there's quite the scandalous story here."

There was a gasp in the room. The front door, which was still open, began flashing with lights from the ground to the top of the door. Macy knew that a senator stepping down would certainly cause a stir, but she couldn't understand why it would call for the paparazzi to come out like hounds. She looked up at Duke. His eyes were now slits of anger. She cast a glance at Kristina and her mouth gaped in shock. There she was, dressed in her pearls that hung down between her breasts and rested peacefully on her perfectly round pregnant belly.

The last thing Duke wanted to do was subject Macy to his former lifestyle. The bulbs were going off. His heart ached at the sight of her face, her eyes wide and glued on Kristina's shape. He cursed under his breath. Macy left his side and stepped away. He reached for her, but she pulled back.

Behind her, Kristina cackled in her menacing way. "Oh dear, Duke, did you find yourself someone to keep you occupied for your time here?" She narrowed her eyes on Macy, her upper lip curled in a jealous rage.

"Sweetie, did he tell you that when he's done here, he's leaving and coming back to me?"

"Get out of here, Kristina," Duke lashed out at the woman standing in the doorway in the center of this mayhem.

"Duke, maybe you and Kristina can talk in the other room," Pablo suggested. Duke didn't miss Monique pinching his arm.

"Or she can just leave," Monique snapped.

"Gee, Monique, I thought we were friends." Kristina's voice lacked conviction.

Monique shrugged her shoulders. "*Duke* is my friend. And that right there—" she pointed toward Kristina's belly "—is some straight-up bullsh—"

"Mo," Pablo hushed her. He wrapped his arm around his wife's shoulder.

"Sorry," Monique mumbled. "But you know you're wrong for coming up here like this."

In desperation to speak with Macy, Duke shook his head no. He looked back around for her, but she was gone. Thinking he spied her being escorted through the kitchen doors by that Lawrence guy, Duke turned an angry stare at Kristina, who was still giggling there, enjoying the spotlight. Choking her right now would not be the right thing to do. The paparazzi were shouting out questions left and right.

"Duke, is that why you left her?"

"Duke, who's the new lady in your life?"

"Duke, are you going to finally marry Kristina now?"

Growling, Duke grabbed Kristina by the elbow and just started walking with her until he found a quiet room. "Gosh, Duke!" Kristina breathed when she looked around. "So quick to get me into bed again?"

They were in a bedroom. There were two twin beds against either side of the wall, and a desk separated them. Posters of Anderson Cooper, Don Lemon, Tavis Smiley and Rachel Maddow covered the walls on one side. Pictures of various baseball teams covered the other. It must have been Gia and MJ's room when they came to stay with their father. Thank God the kids were out on a hayride and weren't being subjected to this drama.

Kristina was sitting on the edge of the bed with its pink comforter, stroking her hand along the material. "It's kind of small, but I'm sure we can make do with it."

"What are you doing here, Kristina?" Duke folded his arms across his chest.

"I came to uncover a story."

"The senator's story or yours?"

She laughed and rolled her eyes. "Don't be silly. Do you think that I wanted things to happen like they did tonight?"

"Of course."

"Well, you're wrong. I'm just doing my job."

"And your job is to come into someone else's home and cause a scene?"

Trying to smile innocently didn't work on Kristina. She was always working an angle somehow. "Now, how could I cause a scene?"

"The paparazzi."

"I can't help it if they follow me everywhere I go."

He snorted. "You could if you didn't tip them off.

I've been here over a month now and I haven't had any trouble from them, and I've been on the news."

"This Podunk town isn't considered news."

Tallahassee had grown on him. Insulting the town was insulting him. His anger grew at her smugness. "If it wasn't news, then you wouldn't be here."

"Well, Oscar thinks…"

He stopped her before she could say anything else about their boss, with whom she'd had an affair. "Does Oscar think that's my child?"

"Of course he does!"

He cursed again, this time not under his breath. "You know this is not possible." He waved his hand at her physical state. The evidence of her affair not only angered him again, but reminded him of what he could not do as a man. The bedroom he stood in reminded him of what another man could do that he couldn't.

Throughout his entire life, he'd competed. He competed in baseball, journalism, and to stay on top of his game at all times. Another man providing a woman with a child was something he could not compete with. It was the one spot in life where he failed. And if he could not create his own family, what did he have to offer Macy?

Kristina pressed her bejeweled hand against her chest. "I know. And you know. And Oscar questions that. But more importantly Oscar's wife doesn't know that."

It had been rumored that Oscar's wife Allegra's family was in the Mafia. Nothing had ever been proven, but the rumors apparently had Kristina scared. "Tell him the truth, Kristina," Duke warned her.

"I can't."

"It's not my problem."

"It kind of is."

He pushed off the wall. "That's not funny."

Kristina picked a fleck of dust off her kneecap as she crossed her legs. Her belly was full. She looked as if she was ready to give birth at any moment. Oscar was crazy for sending her out on a story so close to her due date.

"It is. You know you wouldn't be where you are if it weren't for me."

That wasn't going to help her case. He looked around the room. "You mean in the bedroom of a friend's home in Tallahassee? Don't forget why I am here."

"You're here because you went on a booty bender." She sighed as if she were the bored one. "Some men go through a drinking bender, but you went through women quicker than I go through a pair of shoes."

He snorted at how wrong Kristina was. There was no booty bender or partying. His days were filled with responsibility. He enjoyed being reliable for Gia and MJ. There were no other women for him, only Macy. Duke's heart ached to see her again and talk to her. His mind raced back to Macy. He had to go find her. What could she be thinking right now? He was thankful someone had come earlier to take the kids on a hayride so that they weren't subjected to the circus outside. "I don't have time for this." He reached for the door.

"Are you going to find your girlfriend?"

"Don't bring her into this."

That got her reporting radar going. She straightened

her spine and raised her eyebrows. "So the little sweater girl is your latest thing, eh?"

"Good night, Kristina. I'm sure you can find your way out."

"I guess Sweater Girl knows all about how you got your job in DC."

It sounded like a threat as he was walking out of the room, so Duke stepped back in. "What did you say?"

"Oh." Kristina sighed and shrugged her shoulders. "I just was curious if she knew the truth about how I was the one who discovered you. You were just covering the sports in New York when I met you."

"I was actually doing just fine, Kristina."

"Yeah, but look how you left things in DC. The world will see you as a typical jock running from your responsibilities, leaving his pregnant girlfriend who's done everything possible for him when she's with child."

"Don't try to threaten me, Kristina." Duke shook his head, "because I could easily take this to the public and have you do a DNA test."

"You'd ruin me!" Kristina exclaimed in a panic-stricken voice. "You of all people should know how important our careers are."

"I really do feel sorry for you."

"C'mon, Duke. This can be our last news story together. The ratings have dropped tremendously since your leave of absence. With you resurfacing by my side, you can get a bigger raise for yourself from MET. Don't forget, I know your contract renegotiation is coming up soon."

"It doesn't matter," Duke said.

"Please, Duke. Your absence has only made social media go crazy, waiting for your return to national news. I know with me being pregnant and on camera with you, my return will be just as welcome after I have the baby."

"No."

Kristina sighed while trying to pitch her ideas. "I just need you to go along with this with me for a little while. This is going to be my last news break until I deliver, then I'm going to lie low."

"Not a chance."

"Think about your future, Duke!" Kristina wailed.

For the first time since she showed up, Duke gave her a genuine smile. "That's just it, Kristina. I am."

That wasn't a good enough answer for Kristina. Nothing was good enough until she had her way. She slunk off the edge of the bed. Doing her best seductive cat walk, as seductive as one could be with a huge belly protruding from her body, she came toward him. He straightened his spine. The smell of her overly chemically processed hair wafted to his nose.

She ignored his rigid body language and snaked her arms around his neck, drawing him down for a kiss. The minute their lips touched, Duke felt guilty and disgusted at the same time. He didn't want to push her away due to the baby, so he reached around his neck and pried her snakelike arms from around him.

"Cut it out, Kristina, it's not going to work."

With a high-pitched giggle, Kristina squared her

shoulders and wiped her bottom lip. "Oh, I think it worked out just the way I wanted." She nodded her head to the right of her where the window curtains were drawn open. In the distance, he could see Macy swiftly walking away.

Chapter 8

Walking through the kitchen into the living room, Macy inhaled the sweet smell of her bakery cookie-scented candles. She checked the clock over the mantel. It was after midnight and she'd been home for the past three hours by herself. Lawrence had been kind enough to bring her home after the ruckus, since Duke was obviously so preoccupied.

As she tied the sash around her soft pink robe, common sense told her to blow the candles out. Common sense told her to get into a pair of real pajamas and just go to bed. But there was a nagging voice coming from somewhere inside that told her to give him a few more minutes.

Macy hadn't meant to leave Duke's side, but she'd caught a glimpse out the front door of the hayride coming back. As a child, Macy could never understand how her parents could just dump her off with her grandparents, but after seeing how the paparazzi flocked to the door… She would never want to subject her children to that.

Her mind kept replaying the incident at Mario's. Her heart ached for the pain that woman must have put him through. Duke had looked like death washed over him when he saw her. From what he'd told her, Macy knew things didn't end well with her. Kristina Barclay was certainly a piece of work. There was no doubting that she had seen her walk by the window outside Mario's house. They'd made direct eye contact and upon doing so, Macy had seen the devilish smirk across her face.

Trying to take her mind off seeing the two of them kissing, Macy turned on the television with the remote control. The midnight broadcast of an entertainment news program was already showing a recap from the paparazzi's point of view of Kristina and Duke. From their angle, Macy had a better view of Duke's face. She had felt his tension when she was standing beside him, but from the camera angle she could see it. His face was taut with anger, his lips pressed firmly together, and his eyes had turned a shade of black, soulless black. Macy shivered, reminding her never to get on his bad side…ever.

The idea of Duke being bonded for life to a woman like Kristina Barclay made her blood boil with jealousy. She wanted to scream and punch something. She wanted to fight for her man and she didn't know how to handle her feelings. When Mario's infidelity had been exposed, Macy was ready to move on with her life, without him.

She wanted Duke. But did she have him anymore? Kristina had a part of Duke inside her and Macy had no control of where this would leave her and Duke. She'd seen him with small children. He loved them. He doted on the Baez kids. Hell, he'd even carved a place for himself in Macy's family. But the dose of reality tonight threatened her future with Duke. Things had been so perfect between her and him. Why did Kristina even come down here? Of course, it was to reclaim Duke. Who wouldn't him as part of their family? Was it even possible for Duke to be the father? He'd told her he couldn't have children. In fact, he'd blurted it out during one of their first real conversations.

The clock struck one and woke Macy out of her slight doze. Her heart sank with the realization of the time. Duke still hadn't shown. Had Kristina's kiss meant more to him than she would have thought? Were they now wrapped up in the sheets on his bed? Jealousy was not an emotion Macy was used to having, but she had to decide if that was what she was feeling as she felt the frame of the remote control squeaking in her hand as she crushed it as she thought.

Macy tried to push the thought of him…the two of them…out of her mind. On TV, a nightly talk show host was going on about the season's shopping and preparation for Christmas, which was in just another week. It reminded Macy that Duke's party was on Christmas Eve. She'd had everything ready to go. His guest list was, well, everyone who could come. With the recent explosion of Kristina, she wondered if she would be on the open-invitation list. She clicked off the television, wishing it was just that easy to turn her thoughts of Kristina and Duke out of her mind.

Well, she thought to herself, no matter what...she still had a job to do, and she would still do the best job possible. Deciding to showing the two of them how a true professional should act, Macy sighed and stood up. She blew out the candle wicks, now drenched in the melted wax. Puffs of burning smoke followed her through the living room and the kitchen as she snuffed all the candles. As she walked down the hallway to head upstairs, there was a faint knock at the front door.

Her heart lurched into her rib cage. Instinctively Macy pulled her fingers through her hair. Without having to ask, she knew it was him. Macy opened the door and leaned against the side of it, staring at Duke with all the nonchalance she could muster.

"What are you doing here, Duke?"

"Macy!" he breathed, stepping closer. Obviously he wasn't thinking, either, because he reached for the sides of her face with his large hands and pulled her into a kiss. A deep kiss. She could taste the whiskey on his cool tongue. "You're okay!"

"Of course I'm okay." Macy pulled away but didn't move her hand or hip from the door.

"Are the kids okay?"

She reached her wrist out and pretended to look at a watch that wasn't there. "It's like five hours later, and you're just now asking me this?"

"I'm sorry. Things just got..." Duke straightened.

"Out of hand? Chaotic?" Macy offered for him. He was still in his ugly sweater. She wasn't sure if that was a good thing or not.

"But the kids are okay?"

She sighed. "The kids are fine. We were able to get them to Mario's neighbor before you and your girlfriend made a scene."

"Whoa." Duke dipped his head to look at her. She wouldn't look at him. Instead, she focused on the tip of the tree on his sweater. "Where is this coming from?"

"I saw you two."

He shrugged. "You saw us what?"

"I saw you two kissing." To see if he would deny it or not, Macy finally looked up at him. His mouth twitched with a smile. "You can leave now."

Duke shook his head. "I'm not going anywhere, Macy. We need to talk."

"Really?" She half chuckled with sarcasm. "You left the party with your girlfriend. Your very pregnant girlfriend."

"Ex," he quickly corrected. "And stop trying to get rid of me, Macy."

"Why should I?" Here it came. Her voice cracked. Macy cleared her throat. "Who are we fooling, Duke? I don't belong in your world, and after a night like tonight, you don't belong in mine."

"The hell I don't!" Duke pushed the door open. His large body filled the frame. She watched his large shoulders rise and fall with each controlled breath he took.

Macy found herself walking backward. She knew Duke would never hurt her, but he'd pushed himself into her foyer with such brute force. Her heart skipped a beat. A fire in her belly grew as he stood there looking over her. Since when had she become a sadist? She wasn't sure, but the thought of Duke throwing her over his shoulder right now and taking her to the couch gave her body such a rush that she could feel her lower extremities vibrate with sensation.

"I used to think it was cute the way you would try to push me aside every time you got scared, Macy, but it's really beginning to piss me off." He ranted a few words in Spanish. She was sure he was cursing as he paced back and forth in front of her, raking his hands over his head. "You know what I think?" he finally asked, in English.

"What?"

"I think you're just afraid to lose."

Macy tried not to laugh at that. "Get out of here, Duke. We can talk some other time."

"I'm not leaving until you hear me out," Duke said. "Kristina is not a part of my life, and that baby she's carrying is not mine."

"Why would she say it's yours? Why come down here and make the announcement like that?"

"Because Kristina lives for the drama," he explained. "But I did not get her pregnant."

"But you guys were involved."

"We were. And if she had it her way, we'd be engaged by now with a wedding sponsored by every corporation. If can recall, I left the news desk when all the rumors started about a possible engagement."

She did recall the tabloids speculating about his untimely leave from the news desk and counting all the sightings of Kristina out alone at public events. Macy nodded.

"Don't nod, tell me you believe me," Duke ordered. "You need to hear me when I say that I, in no way, shape or form, am involved with any of Kristina's scheming. The only person I care about is you. Do I make myself clear?"

A flash of excitement coursed through her veins. Was he choosing her? "Yes."

"Yes, what?" he asked.

Macy rolled her eyes. "Yes, I understand there is nothing between you and Kristina."

"And?"

"Duke, it's late."

"That's fine with me." Duke stopped pacing and glared at her. Her breath got caught in the back of her throat as she noticed the look in his eyes.

She shook her head in disbelief at the audacity of his intentions. "You can't be serious," she said as his mouth paused a millimeter before her lips.

"Very."

Without having a chance to react, Macy fell into Duke's embrace. He had one hand at the back of her neck while the other snaked around her waist, his thumb massaging the tie of her robe open. She'd been ready for this. She'd been waiting for this. The apex of her thighs began to melt with fire. Duke bent her backward. Inches from the ground, she gazed at the ceiling as his mouth began to open her robe. She could feel his grin when he discovered her naked underneath.

As one of his large hands still held her back in his arms, his other pulled open the robe completely, which pooled around his hand where he supported her back. There she was, bare, vulnerable for him to see. Duke took a caressing finger from her bottom lip down, over her chin, down her chest and between her breasts. She felt her body quiver as his fingers reached the curls down below.

"You are so beautiful," he whispered into her ear just before nibbling on her earlobe.

Macy struggled to stand up.

He shook his head. "Let me just feast on you right now."

She thought she'd said yes. The words couldn't form, but at least a sound of approval escaped her throat. She sucked in a breath of cold air when he took a nipple into his mouth; first one, then the other, then both at the same time, balancing her breasts in his large hands. Aimlessly, she reached for the sweater encasing him. She tugged at the material. Duke grinned and maneuvered her to the steps. He pulled the sweater over his head. The gold cross hanging from his chest blended in with his golden-brown skin and twinkled against the last of the candles Macy hadn't blown out yet.

Duke moved his bare torso between her naked legs and brought his mouth down on hers. He revived her with his kisses. He was so warm against her. So full of life against her. Her hands wrapped around his shoulders. Her fingertips splayed across the muscles of his back, down toward the waistline of his jeans. Moving her fingers around, she fumbled with the buckle. She couldn't quite pull the button from the hole and had to lean back to get a view of what she was doing. She cast a glance up at Duke, who was looming over her with his arms on either side of her. He inhaled deeply.

"I'm not going to let our first time together be right here on the steps."

Disappointment ripped through her. She was sure, as she slid his pants over his tailbone, that she could change his mind. "Really?"

"Really," he said, lifting her by her bottom and placed her up two steps. "You're going to lead me to your bedroom."

"I am?" She mocked him with as much bravado as she could. "How do you expect me to…" Her words once again were lost in her throat as he dipped his head between her legs, his tongue like a heat-seeker, and found her center.

"Oh. My…" Macy moaned at the feel of his vibrating tongue. She tried to think of baseball cards or cooking recipes—anything to keep her from coming so soon. His tongue slipped into her center, stretching her almost. She quivered and took deep breaths. The only way she could stop from exploding right now was to go up one more step. But with each step she inched up, Duke was right there, his lips pressing against her lower ones until she made it to the top step.

"Which room?"

"Th-there," Macy moaned breathlessly.

Duke swept her up into his arms and took her quickly to her bedroom. He placed her squarely on the bed and kicked out of his pants.

A few hours ago, Macy had been ready for this. She had candles going in her room. The chiffon mosquito netting was drawn on three sides of the bed already. Duke took a knee slowly onto the bed. Macy lay on her back and propped herself up by her elbows. She stretched her toe against his chest. Duke turned and pressed the high arch of her inner foot to his mouth and kissed it.

He was built like a Latin god. He had the world's most beautiful broad shoulders, tapered waist, six-pack abs and powerful thighs, not to mention the world's most beautiful erection staring right at her. He was playing with something in his hands. Macy glanced down briefly and noticed the foil wrapper. The realization of what they were about to do hit her. It excited her. She wasn't ready to stop looking at him. Her mouth watered at the sight of him. She sat up farther until she was on her knees and knelt in front of him.

She could feel him shiver as she pressed her lips against his. His hands stroked through her hair down to the small of her back and around her belly. He reached between her legs and felt her ripeness. She was going to die if she didn't have him right now. Macy reached down for his erection and took it in her hands. He was hard as steel and smooth as velvet at the same time. The tip of his head leaked slightly with evidence he was just as ready for her.

She pulled away from her kiss and raised one eyebrow at him, daring him to make the next move. "You've got me in my room. Now what..." Macy wasn't sure if she got the enunciation of the *t* out of her mouth before

Duke had grabbed her by her knees and flipped her on her backside again. She lifted her head to laugh and was greeted by his soft mouth nibbling on her bottom lip as he swiftly entered her body.

Her bones in her ankles crackled as she wrapped them around his waist as he drove into her. His body kept such a steady, fast pace she was sure they had run the Kentucky Derby at least four times by now. Duke extended one leg over his shoulder and drove home into her. Her breasts bounced rapidly and wildly. He took a nipple into his mouth as he took the other leg and threw it over his other shoulder. Macy braced one hand down on the mattress under her contorted body. The other hand pulled against the back of his neck.

Duke broke off kissing her breasts and growled. It was primal. It was erotic. Apparently, he felt all the sexual frustrations she'd been experiencing with him, and they both were finally able to let it out. And she did. Her body stumbled with a twitch and Duke moved, if possible, even faster, all the way out and powerfully back in again.

"Let it out," he whispered in her ear.

She released her scream with the first orgasm. Duke was right behind her, groaning louder and louder, until they both hit the peak of their climaxes at the same time. Chills spread all the way down Macy's body. She'd never experienced such a thing. It was the most beautiful thing ever.

It wasn't until they heard the sound of a sanitation truck coming down the street that they got out of the bed. Macy hadn't realized how tired she was. She also didn't realize that she had literally spent all night long making love to this beautiful man. They lay in her bed, their hands entwined.

"Please let me explain what happened this evening."

"I don't want to talk about it."

Duke turned on his side. Even though the candles had burned themselves out hours ago, Macy still knew Duke was looking at her. "You don't want to talk about what we just did?"

"Oh…that's what you wanted to talk about?"

"I used a condom with you, Macy."

"I know." She felt herself blush. "I think I remember putting it on you." She'd never been the one to do it before, but she'd seen enough episodes of *Real Sex* to know how to do it.

"It wasn't because I was worried about getting you pregnant."

"I know, Duke." Macy lay on her side and stroked his biceps, remembering Serena had said what big muscles he had. Her hand barely made it around one side of his arm.

"But you saw Kristina…"

Macy sighed into the darkness. "When you first came to the office, you told me that you had a serious illness as a child, resulting in you not being able to have kids."

"You remembered that?"

"Of course. I also remember you saying how Kristina betrayed you. It didn't take a genius to figure the rest out."

"No, I guess not."

"But I appreciate you trying to protect me tonight anyway." She scooted closer. "But don't think I appreciated seeing you two kiss."

"You were spying?"

"I would hardly call it spying when I was trying to get all the kids returning from the hayride to go to Mario's neighbors' and there you two were."

She felt the bed shift with his weight as he raised himself on his elbows. "I would hardly call that kissing her."

"And don't get me started on the circus at the door." She mimicked his movements and struggled to sit up. She started to turn on the light by her bedside, but realized that for the past few hours she'd been sweating up a storm. She must look a mess. The cameras tonight reminded Macy of Duke's glamorous world. She imagined everyone in it woke up flawless. "I can't imagine living under that kind of scrutiny."

"I never liked it."

"Then why did you put up with that?"

"It was just part of…" His voice trailed off into the darkness.

"It was what Kristina wanted," Macy summed up. She felt him nod. "It seems like you did a lot of things that she wanted." She thought about his situation with Kristina. From what she'd learned over the past few weeks, Duke owed a lot to Kristina. She wanted him to do the news; he did the news. She wanted to move to DC; he moved to DC. He made plans to visit his parents in the DR, and she didn't want to, so he didn't go.

Obviously, she wanted to put her pregnancy on him. What was he going to do?

"So…" Macy slowly drawled out. "What did she want?"

"Well, she wants me to go along with this pregnancy."

"What the hell?" She sounded jealous. But she couldn't stop herself. "You're going to let this lie continue?"

"I told her no."

"Why did she even feel she could ask that of you?"

"Macy," Duke sighed. "The baby isn't mine."

"And I clearly understand it's not yours," Macy clipped icily. "Why does Kristina think she can come to you and ask you to cover for her if you two have been over for a while now?"

"It's because of who the father of the baby is," Duke confessed. "Look, a part of me had gone along with Kristina's path. There was a time we both wanted the same thing. We both wanted to report the news. We both achieved that. I owe my success to a handful of people."

In the darkness, he reached for her, turning her body to its side, and pressed his against hers. "You know I'm under contract MET right now in DC, and it's my outstanding reputation as a news anchor that gives me leverage with the contract there and keeps me here in Tallahassee. I like having the upper hand when I come to a table to negotiate. Shaming or exposing Kristina won't help."

"And what about the giant elephant in the room?"

"Huh?"

"Her pregnancy, Duke."

"Well, you already know that it's not mine."

"True." She didn't like the sound of his voice.

"So to me, that's all that matters."

She sighed against the pillow. Her heart sank at his explanation. She would have much rather preferred he told Kristina to go to hell rather than let the world believe that it was his child she was carrying. She wondered what it was she had over him to make him think he had to protect her. That urge of jealousy struck her again. She wondered what that feeling would be like if Duke had been so protective over her.

A flash of panic wrenched at her heart. Tears pooled in the corners of her eyes. She realized right then and there that she loved Duke Rodriguez. And the heartbreaking thing was that he obviously did not feel the same way about her. Not once in his speech about his career and his negotiations had he mentioned her or the direction of their relationship. Kristina was a part of building Duke's career. What did Macy offer him for his future?

Macy controlled her breathing so that Duke couldn't feel her sob. Fortunately the garbage trucks down the street grew closer, drowning out any sound she might have made. She pulled the covers away.

"Where are you going?" he asked, holding her close.

"The garbage trucks are coming. If I don't get the trash out now, it will be doubled next week, and they're not picking up the day before Christmas, as usual."

Duke raised himself up on his elbow. "Well, hang on. I'll do that."

Macy pushed him back with her shoulder. "It's okay. I know where everything is. I'll be right back. You rest."

"We can sleep in, you know."

How well did she know that? Duke didn't have to do the news in the morning. She knew his schedule by heart. Weekends were his free time, which he spent helping her. But then Monday would roll around and of course, this Monday would be different. This Monday, he'd be working with Kristina. "I know. But I'll be right back. You get some rest."

The coolness of the sheets as he reached for Macy's soft and tender frame woke Duke from his slumber. The realization of what they'd done up until the wee hours of the morning began to register in his brain. He was more in love with Macy now than ever before. She was everything he'd imagined. And he couldn't wait to tell her.

Duke sat up in bed and looked around for any sign of her. He found her discarded robe neatly hung up against the back of the bedroom door. His jeans were folded on the edge of the bed. Reaching for them, Duke slipped them on and looked around for his shoes. The sun was already spilling into the room from the open curtains. The clock on her nightstand said it was eight. He'd slept in. But that was okay; he didn't have to go in to the station today.

He sniffed the air, expecting the faint hint of coffee or bacon or eggs, something. Not that he expected Macy to make breakfast or anything, but after a night like last night, he was sure if she wasn't in the bed with him when they woke up, she would be down in the kitchen.

She always had food ready to serve whenever he got off work and came directly over.

"Macy?" Duke called out, opening the bedroom door. He looked around the room before leaving. His sweater from last night had fallen on the floor by the bed. It was too warm to put it back on, so he buttoned up the top button on his pants and trotted down the stairs, anxious to see Macy again.

Walking down the steps, his heart raced as he remembered the details of what had happened there. He was smiling to himself when he reached the bottom step and walked down the hallway. He heard shuffling in the kitchen and decided he would surprise her. The surprise was on him.

"Am I interrupting?" Duke asked. His smile faded at the sight of Macy and her friend Lawrence huddled together against her counter. Macy was dressed casually in a pair of pink velour jogging pants and a plain white T-shirt. Her hair was pulled up into a ponytail at the top of her head. She smiled, but it wasn't a full smile. Something was wrong, he realized as she tucked a stray hair behind her ear. Her cheeks were flushed. Duke's eyes darted back to Lawrence, who shared the same embarrassed look. The hairs on the back of his neck rose.

Moving from Macy's side, Lawrence crossed the kitchen and extended his hand toward Duke. "Hey, man, I was just leaving."

"Don't leave on my account," Duke said casually as he firmly shook the man's hand.

"Oh, it's not that. I've just got, um…some errands

to run." Lawrence stepped backward, reached for some papers on the counter and then fumbled with them, rolling and putting them in the back pocket of his jeans. Duke thought the man's skintight white T-shirt was a bit much for eight in the morning, but chose to ignore it. He had to remind himself that even though the two of them worked closely together once, Macy was with him. Last night had confirmed that. "Congratulations on winning."

"Winning?"

"The—uh." Lawrence shifted his glance to Macy. It was a guilty look. Macy said they'd gone out a few times, but that there were no sparks. There certainly seemed to be sparks right now. Both their faces were flushed. "The ugly sweater contest."

Duke looked down at himself, knowing his chest was bare. The child in him flexed his pec muscles. "Oh. Yeah. Thanks."

"Well. Macy, I'll see you later?"

"Yeah, sure," Macy said, folding her arms across her chest. Duke could see the swelling of her breasts, and now that he'd had a taste of them, he didn't want to share with anyone, ever. "I'll walk you out."

"Oh, don't worry," Lawrence said nervously. "I can show myself out."

In his years as a reporter, Duke had come across some shady people. Grown men stuttering and stumbling over themselves was a telltale sign that something wasn't right. Lawrence was in too much of a rush to get out of there. It was just like the time he'd walked into Oscar's office and Oscar and Kristina had flown to opposite sides of the room like the Red Sea parting. He knew it was wrong to compare the two situations. Macy was nothing like Kristina. But there was still that nagging feeling in the back of his head. If Kristina could fool him, especially with the paparazzi always following her around, surely Macy could...

"Are you hungry?" Macy asked, breaking him from his morbid thoughts.

In an instant, Duke's thoughts went from morbid to desirous. He wanted nothing more than to place Macy on top of that counter. Every inch of his body went hard. His hand went to his growling stomach, but he wasn't hungry for food.

Macy's eyes followed his hand and then went back up to his face. Her dark eyes sparkled as they crinkled when she smiled. "You can't be serious."

"Oh, I'm very serious." Duke moved across the kitchen floor, enjoying the way Macy's throat moved up and down as she gulped. She braced herself against the counter, which was fine with him. He gently picked her up and sat her on the countertop. Their hips met. He stiffened instantly.

Wedging her hand against his chest, Macy created some space between them. "Wait, as much as I'd love to do this..."

Duke listened as he planted a trail of kisses against her neck.

"We can't. I've got some things to take care of."

"Like what?" Duke placed another kiss against the side of her mouth, purposely not brushing her succulent lips. If she wanted a kiss, she was going to have to turn her face for it.

"You're not making this easy."

"It's not supposed to be easy." Duke took hold of her hands and pulled them down to his waistband. "It's hard."

She blushed. He wasn't looking, but he could feel the heat from her cheeks as he nibbled on her ear.

"No, seriously. I have work to do."

"No, you don't. The judging went on last night." He continued kissing her earlobe. Little goose bumps appeared on her shoulder blade and arm.

Macy sucked in her breath. "I'm serious, Duke."

The sound in her voice was serious. Duke straightened up, but didn't move from between her legs. "Is it the Lawrence guy?"

"Wh-what?"

She stuttered. Duke's heart sank. It was the same stutter he'd heard once before. He looked into Macy's dark eyes for as long as he let her, which wasn't long before she looked and pushed him away. "That Lawrence guy. He was here pretty early in the morning."

"He's a friend of mine."

"Really?" Duke regretted folding his arms across his chest the minute he said the words. But it was too late. His tone and Macy's response had put them both in combative mode. He had to fix this. "I'm sorry, it's just…"

"It's just nothing," Macy snapped.

Too late, he thought. She was already squaring her

shoulders for battle. Duke raked his hands over his head. "Let's start this morning over."

Macy shook her head from side to side. Her lips were already flattened in anger. "No, that's quite all right. We might as well go and finish this."

"What is *this*?" Duke threw his hands up, still trying to surrender. His heart slammed against his rib cage in panic. Quickly he softened his voice. "I don't want to fight with you, Macy, especially after last night."

"Ohhh," cooed a voice behind them.

Duke cursed inwardly and turned around to see Serena leaning against the door frame. Her bright face was lit up with a quizzical grin. "Good morning, Duke, Macy. I didn't mean to interrupt, but the door was unlocked and I thought you'd want to see the results from the contest for the best decorated home."

Glancing back and forth at him and then her boss, Serena extracted a paper from the oversize bag on her shoulder. "You're upset." She noticed. "Maybe you've already seen it."

Now next to him, Macy shook her head. "No, not yet."

"Macy," Duke breathed. "We need to talk."

"I can come back," Serena offered.

"No." "Yes, please." Duke and Macy spoke at the same time. His eyes pleaded with Serena. "Will you at least give us a few minutes?"

"Don't tell her what to do," Macy interjected. "Serena, stay."

Confused, Serena looked between them again. She bit her bottom lip. "Well, since Duke is topless…"

"Serena," Macy warned.

"Fine, fine." Serena handed Macy the paper. "How about I just go sit out on the deck for a few minutes while you two talk?"

Macy took the paper, but shook her head as she scanned over the front page.

"Can you put that down, Macy? We need to talk."

"Why do we need to talk, Duke? I said I was busy."

"Busy doing what?"

Her eyes narrowed on his.

She cocked her head to the side in order to reexamine him. "Oh, you think because of last night that I am supposed to bend to your will?"

"That's not what I'm saying." Duke paused with his brows furrowing. "What is going on here?"

"Obviously, *this* is going on," Macy held up the paper for him.

There on the front page of the *Tallahassee Daily* was Duke's picture at the precise moment he was ushering Kristina off into the bedroom. Considering he'd done basically the same thing to her this morning, it wasn't a good look.

"Macy, I explained that..."

"Kids talk, Duke. How do I explain this to Gia? What do I say to MJ when his friends ask him about you being in a relationship with me, while this woman is claiming you're the father of her child on national TV?"

He scratched his head. "But I already told you I'm not."

Macy shook the paper at him. "Which means nothing

when this is plastered in the news. Jesus, Duke! What am I supposed to do now?"

"Nothing," Duke said, trying to control his irritation at Kristina. Damn her for coming back. "It will blow over."

"It will blow over with the two of you reporting the news together?"

"Now wait a minute…"

"No," Macy cut him off. "I'm not going to wait a minute while you figure everything out."

"Hold on now, Macy… I dropped the whole issue with Lawrence being in here so early in the morning."

"What?" She gasped with laughter. "You can't be serious about throwing that in my face when you have a pregnant girlfriend who you have to work with…"

"*Ex!*" he interjected. She shook the paper again at him as if that made a difference. He couldn't help what the paper wrote. He couldn't control it. "Okay, I think I see what's going on here, Macy."

The room grew quiet while Macy stood there, waiting for him to explain.

"You don't like the idea of me and Kristina working together. I understand that. But I think what it is, is that you're just afraid."

"Afraid?" she choked out.

"Yes," Duke replied matter-of-factly. "This morning you saw how good things could be for us, and you're just trying to push me away."

"Why would I do that?"

"I don't know why, but you've been pushing me away since we met. And you know what I think?"

"What?" she asked drily, with a sigh.

"I think you're afraid of a challenge."

Scoffing at him, Macy tossed the paper on the table. "What?"

"You're afraid of a challenge. Just think about the homes you did, homes you've won awards for. You don't like dealing with difficult people. You didn't like dealing with the Wainwrights. You didn't like their new ways of doing things and figured you would lose the contest if you worked with them. You don't want to work with me because you're afraid you'll lose me. Think about it, Macy…you're a sore loser."

"Are you calling me a loser?"

He sighed with deeply felt frustration. Counting to ten backward in Spanish, he shook his head. "That's not what I'm saying."

"Well, you're wrong about the contest. It's not about winning. It's about what I won. And it doesn't really matter because I did not win this year." With that, Macy snatched the paper back up and held it in his face. Her fingers pointed toward the small article at the bottom of the page. Duke could clearly see that the winning house was not hers. Instead, there was a proud middle-aged couple standing in front of a uniquely decorated home. He could only assume they were the Wainwrights. Macy set the paper back down and brushed past him. She stopped at the doorway. "But you're right about one thing—I don't like dealing with difficult people. You can show yourself out."

"Macy." Duke pleaded, "Don't be like this. We still have work to do together."

"Don't worry about it. I'll still do your party on Christmas Eve. But I don't want to look at your face until then."

Duke stood in the kitchen. He cringed when he heard a door slam and cursed when he realized it was the front door. Had she really left? Baffled, Duke turned around. Serena was now back at the doorway, shaking her head.

"What just happened here?" he asked her. If anyone should know, it had to be Serena.

"It seems as though the two of you had a fight."

"That was more than just a fight," Duke said, trying to steady his voice. "Did you have to show her the morning paper?"

Serena shrugged. "I really didn't come over here to show her the article about you and that Kristina woman. I came over here to see how she was doing since she lost the Christmas decoration contest."

"Is she really that much of a sore loser?"

"Duke, it was never about her winning."

Duke nodded his head. "She said that. So what's it about?"

"It's about the money she would have won," Serena said, then she shook her head. "Or more about where it goes when she wins."

"So where does it go?"

"To the Child Victim Fund for kids who have lost both their parents."

Duke's mouth dropped open. He felt like a world-class ass.

Chapter 9

"Well, you're absolutely miserable without him," Serena commented, standing in the doorway of the department store changing room.

Looking in the three-way mirror, Macy shook her head at Serena's reflection. The morning of Duke's holiday party was girl time at the mall. Monique brought Maylen along with Lucia because the baby hadn't been feeling well lately, and Mo wanted to keep an eye on her. Macy brought Gia, who insisted that Serena come. Serena had to come along to give her two cents whenever necessary. After brunch, Gia took Maylen to get their nails done while the older women tried on clothes. Lucia was so tired just from the ride over to the mall that she'd fallen asleep in her stroller, giving Monique a chance to try on a few dresses, as well.

In a skintight black velvet dress that showed off a figure that would rival any pinup girl, Mo stood next to Serena and was nodding at her comment. "She's right, you know."

Macy was trying on a dress. The bench in the changing room was filled with different dresses in different styles and different colors. Nothing seemed right. She only needed to look at her friends' frowning faces each time she opened the door to know that each dress wasn't the right one. If it didn't hug her body too tight, it made her look too matronly. It had been a week since she had that horrible falling-out with Duke. He had the nerve to question her friendship with Lawrence when he was going to allow the world to think that he was the father of Kristina's unborn child. She knew that the whole thing with Lawrence could easily have been cleared up with a logical explanation, but with the way he reacted toward her, he didn't deserve one. But it still didn't help how she was feeling now. What her friends were telling her was the truth.

She not only looked miserable, but she felt miserable, as well. Every morning she woke up with her heart feeling heavy. It ached. Duke had spent only one night in her bed and already her sheets felt empty and cold without him.

"Thanks a lot," she said drily into the mirror.

"It's Christmas Eve," Monique said cheerfully. "And tonight you get to see Duke after your ban…"

"I didn't *ban* him exactly," Macy quickly said.

Serena snickered. "It sure sounded like it to me."

"Either way," Monique said, laughing, "I know he can't wait to see you."

Duke had honored Macy's wishes by not trying to see her for a week. It gave her time to think. Perhaps working closely together since Thanksgiving had blurred her thoughts. She needed space, and this time apart allowed her to prepare for Duke's party. But she couldn't secretly help but wish he would have disregarded her banishment. If he was so eager to see her, he would have just come over, no matter what she said. And being the stubborn person she knew she was, she wasn't about to see him before tonight.

Since she knew his hours at the station, Macy was able to get in and out of his house when he wasn't there. Everything was set for his big party this evening. She hadn't kept track of who was coming, since it was an open invitation to the whole town. Macy banked on a lot of families not trying to come, thinking it was already going to be full. She also banked on the fact that it was Christmas Eve and most families already had plans. Macy had every caterer in town on call. She figured a few hundred orders of everyone's best dishes on the hour would keep the steady flow of guests satisfied.

Macy smiled at Monique and nodded toward her gown. "I like that dress for you. If you're not careful, you and Pablo are going to have another baby before the year is up."

"Are you ignoring what I'm saying?"

"Of course not," Macy said in a sarcastic tone. "Look, this time apart for Duke and me is good."

"Good how?" Monique and Serena chorused.

"Good because this is the way things are going to be when he leaves," Macy said with a shrug. She ran her fingers along the bustline of the red dress as she looked in the mirror at herself. She missed Duke desperately. She missed seeing his dimples when he grinned at her. She missed hearing his deep voice with its heavy accent when he was trying to be charming. She missed hearing about Mao.

But Macy also thought about the brighter side of Duke not being around her.

This week, she was able to get in and out of stores without someone stopping the two of them for Duke's autograph. Of course, while the hounding in public ceased, the hounding from her children increased when she came home from work. MJ and Gia wanted to know where Duke was and when he was coming back. *It is better this way*, she told herself.

"But he said he was going to come back and see you," Serena griped. Trying as hard as she might, Serena's efforts to get Macy to talk to Duke weren't working out. If there was a problem or a concern dealing with Duke's party, Macy made Serena handle it. Serena had tried to flake out on a meeting with Duke, but Macy had been one step ahead of her. She had to be one step ahead. If she wasn't, she would have easily fallen back in with Duke and not been able to resist his charm. She needed to stay strong.

"Sure, he would come back to visit, but I'm not sure I'm the stop-by-and-visit type of girl." Macy sighed. "Seeing how the paparazzi went crazy with him at Mario's party gave me an insight on what it really would be like to get involved with Duke."

Monique sighed impatiently. "You're already involved with him."

"And it's not better," Serena said. "You're slamming things around the house. You're moody. Andy and Spencer said they feel like they need to walk on eggshells around you."

"It really is," Macy argued with her friends. "Duke and I are in two different worlds. He was just taking a break from his celebrity life and I just happened to be a part of it."

Monique shook her head and *tsk*ed at her. "The paparazzi were here because Kristina called them. Duke had been here for almost six weeks and he hadn't been hounded like that. So it's not really a true experience of what life with him would be like."

"It is true," Macy countered. "Duke was here because he was getting into some pretty bad stuff, partying, drinking and whatever, and Pablo brought him down here to clear out his head. He was just here taking a break."

"That doesn't mean he hasn't fallen in love with you, Macy," Monique said.

"It doesn't mean that he *has*, either. He hasn't really said it, you know." Macy wasn't sure if that's what hurt the most—that she was supposed to stand by his side while he allowed this farce with Kristina to continue, or that she didn't know how he really felt about her?

"So if he said he loved you, would you reconsider things?" Serena asked.

"Well, if he said it right now, it would just be staged and not real." Macy shook her head back and forth as her friends groaned in frustration. She chewed her bottom lip for a brief second before she confessed her problem. "Do you guys realize that she wants him to go along with the charade, saying that the baby she's carrying is his?"

"That bitch!" Serena exclaimed, balling her fists against her hips. "Girl, just let me have one minute alone with her. I'll get her straight."

Macy shook her head. "As much as I wouldn't mind that, it still wouldn't help the situation. Duke's kindness to Kristina affects my family."

"But you have to realize, Kristina knows her career is washed up. She was nothing without Duke," Monique was saying. Macy had learned through Monique that since the Tallahassee station, WKSS, was an affiliate of her DC station, Kristina was allowed to be the guest anchorwoman. While Macy couldn't bring herself to watch Duke on television last week, she was glad to hear that Kristina was reporting the news from the field instead of right next to Duke. "But you know, I can understand that you have Gia and MJ to protect." Monique nodded her blond head, beginning to understand.

"Gia knows what's going on. She has already had enough people at school Tweeting her to find out what's happening, because everyone at school was getting to know Duke as the coach's helper, and that Gia was responsible for bringing him there. And now all that's going to change. He's going to leave." Macy inhaled deeply. If she thought about it anymore, she would start crying again. Sadly, she shook her head and reached for the doors. "Let me get out of this dress and find the right one. This one is too long."

As she closed the doors, Serena called out over the top of the door, "So if you're so sure things are going to end between you and Duke, why are you in search of the perfect dress?"

"Because even though he's leaving, I want him to see what he's going to miss."

On the other side of the door, she heard Monique and Serena agree with her reasons. She slipped out of the dress she was trying on and back into her jeans and black sweater. She flipped her hair out from her collar when she heard Gia and Maylen panting as they ran into the dressing room. There was a slight panic when she opened the door and saw both girls faces' were bright red. They were both speaking at once. Monique was trying to calm Maylen down.

"What is going on?"

"We found the perfect dress for you, Mom!" Gia cried.

"Okay, fine, let's go find it. Hang on, let me find my…"

Gia pulled on her arm. "We don't have time. It's Christmas Eve and there's one dress left and we got to get it before someone else buys it for tonight."

"Fine. Fine." Macy shook her head and laughed as Gia and Maylen guided her down the corridor of the top floor of the mall. They'd gotten there first thing in the morning, and it wasn't that busy. Now it seemed like people were everywhere. She started to understand the urgency and picked up her pace.

Behind her, Serena was laughing. Monique was running as she pushed Lucia in the stroller. They had to look like a sight. They stopped short in front of a little boutique, Desideri. From what Macy knew of the store, its wares rivaled Victoria's Secret lingerie. It catered to women of all sizes. Macy stood at the entrance, glancing up at the fancy black letters, then back down at her teenage daughter. She cocked her eyebrow. "What do *you* know about this place?"

"I Tweeted that I was at the mall with my mom who was looking for a dress. My friend Michaela's sister works here and says she has the perfect dress for you."

"How does she even know what my size is?"

"She saw you on the news at Daddy's stupid Ugly Sweater Party and knew exactly what you needed to shut Kristina Barclay up."

Great, the whole world's first impression of her was in that ugly sweater. *Damn Mario!* "I can't go in there. They sell lingerie." Macy clutched her heart and feigned outrage. "I am a mother."

"And clothes," Serena said, catching up to them. "I've been in here once or twice. C'mon…I'm sure we'll find something."

The curvy mannequins in the window were all wearing seductive satin or lace. Macy would have thought that pushing the clothing up front would have been a better idea. But she took going in there with a grain of salt. She needed a dress.

"Serena!" A tall, curvaceous woman beamed coming from behind the counter. "It's been a while."

"The saleslady knows your name?" Monique mumbled, amused.

Ignoring her, Serena stretched out her arms and gave the woman a hug and an air kiss on both cheeks. "I know, but I haven't had a good date in a while. Claire, these are my friends Macy and Monique, and their girls, Gia, Maylen and Lucia."

"I'm Michaela's friend," Gia said, extending her hand to the saleslady.

"The Tweet," said Claire. "I do have the perfect dress."

"Thank God," Gia breathed. Without hesitation, Claire grabbed Macy by the wrist and led her to the small dark pink dressing rooms in the back of the store. "It's already hanging up in the back. I know it's the perfect one."

"Well…thanks." Macy stumbled into the dressing room and found what looked like the perfect black dress. Judging from the length of the material hanging from the hanger, she expected it to stop short enough on her legs without making her look like too much of a schoolmarm or too much like an extra from one of those trashy reality shows. She worried about the spaghetti straps and the sweetheart top, but once she tried the dress on, she fell in love.

Outside of the dressing room, a commotion began to take place. Macy poked her head out to see that Kristina Barclay and her entourage of paparazzi had waltzed into Desideri unceremoniously. The photographers were capturing Kristina picking up various garments and splaying them across her belly to see if they would fit.

"You all can't be in here," Claire explained to them. "No cameras. The owners are very serious about that."

"Don't be silly. I'm Kristina Barclay," Kristina cooed.

"I know, but…" Claire tried to get a word in.

"And I'm here to get a dress for an important event this evening. I'm sure the owner, Gabrielle Owens, wouldn't mind. We've met several times, you know."

Not ready to step out of the dressing room yet, Macy watched her daughter's reaction. The material of the dress, firm as it was to keep anything from jiggling, hung around her waist. With her little fists balled up, Gia started to go into action, but Monique protectively stood in front of her. "Kristina, perhaps you can find someplace else to shop. I happen to know Gabrielle Owens Brutti *personally*, and I know she wouldn't appreciate your cameras in here."

As if on cue, Lucia stirred in her stroller with a gurgling sound. Kristina's face faltered for a moment for the camera, trying not to let Monique's words of truth hit her. She spied Lucia in her stroller. "Oh, is this the little one? I can't wait to have mine." She touched her belly. "Any day now, you know. And *we're* so excited."

There was no need for an explanation of who she meant by *we're*. But one of the paparazzi asked about Duke's whereabouts for the day and if Kristina was there to pick out a dress to surprise him at tonight's party. Macy seethed with an anger and possessiveness she didn't think she had the right to have. Duke might have explained what the deal was to her, but not the whole world. And right now, anyone listening would fall for the lies of Kristina's tale. Kristina sidestepped the questions with vague comments about surprising everyone tonight. Then, without asking, she reached down and picked up Lucia. Lucia opened her light brown eyes, took one look at the woman who was holding her, then to her mother and then back at Kristina, and promptly threw up. As much fuss as Kristina made coming in, she made the same, if not more, going out. She screamed in disgust as she rushed down the corridor. *Lucia the hero*, Macy thought. She made a mental note to kiss the baby for giving Kristina what she deserved.

Finally fully dressed, Macy walked out of the dressing room, and the boutique erupted with laughter. Subconsciously, Macy wrapped her arms around her shoulders. In the mirror, she thought the dress had fit like a glove but still managed to hide her bulges. The black straps came close to her shoulder, exposing much of her breasts. When she was looking in the mirror, she thought she'd looked sexy and sophisticated at the same time. She thought it had been perfect.

"Does it look that bad?"

"Oh, Mommy!" Gia gasped, spinning around. Her dark eyes lit up with excitement. "It's perfect!"

"She's right," Monique said, shuffling Lucia in her arms. "You look beautiful."

"That's definitely the one," Serena agreed.

"Then what were you guys laughing at?" She tucked a stray hair behind her ear, pretending not to know what had happened.

Gia held her phone in the air. "Check your Tweets when you get a chance."

"Otherwise, stay tuned for the evening news!" Monique wrapped her free arm around Gia's shoulders. "Honey, that dress is the one. Get it and let's get ready for the party of the year."

"So let me get this straight," Mario said, setting his beer on the counter in Duke's kitchen. "You thought for a second that there was something still going on between me and Macy? And then you thought there was something going on between Macy and Lawrence?"

As much as Duke hated talking about his private life with the man who once shared a life with Macy, he did. He sighed and picked up his own beer. He had a living room filled with guests who'd arrived early. Fortunately, Macy had the hindsight to have the caterers begin an hour earlier. He had been dressed in just a towel when they set up the first dishes. He had to admit that he was extremely disappointed when it hadn't been Macy at the door.

He'd abided by her wishes, giving her a week to think about things. It gave him a chance to get things in order, as well. Every day that he came home from work, he knew she'd been there. Not only could he smell her coconut scent, but he could see the differences her preparation had made in his home. She cleared out all of the furniture in the downstairs rooms and had a huge Douglas fir in the corner of one room. The large twelve-seat table had been taken out of the dining room and in its place she put several dozen tall round tables around which people could stand and eat the food.

The woman of the hour still hadn't shown up. Duke sought solace in his kitchen. Mario had done the same.

But Duke figured it was better access to the food coming in from the back door delivery and better access to the female servers to gather the food without running into the guests.

"Well, when you say it like that, I know I came off insecure."

"Yeah, you did," Mario said. "And I ain't messin' with you this time. You got this other chick Kristina pregnant."

Duke shook his head. "It's not my baby. I know that, Kristina knows that and more importantly, Macy knows that."

"Now, see, that's where you're wrong. My kids are involved in this. How do you think it looks for Gia or MJ? Do you think they would understand something like this?"

In the past days, he had time to think; Duke screwed things up. He thought that, as long as Macy knew the truth, everything would be okay. But Kristina not correcting the public misconception on who the father of her baby was had damaged everything Duke had built with Macy, Gia and MJ. "I am going to fix this."

Mario said, "I kind of took care of it for you."

Not knowing what Mario would do, Duke felt dread wash over him. "What did you do?"

"Excuse me, Duke," Serena said, poking her head in the doorway. Duke's feeling of impending doom went away, because if Serena was around, that had to mean that Macy was nearby, as well. Macy had pawned Serena off on him all week long. Every time he called Winter Paradise to ask a question or verify a charge,

Serena tried giving the phone to Macy, but he could hear Macy turn the call down. It was sad that just hearing Macy's voice had cheered him up a bit.

"Santa will be flying in soon. Are you ready?"

"Santa?" Duke asked with a raised eyebrow. "Flying in?"

"Yes, didn't you look at your itinerary?" Serena grinned.

He shook his head. "No."

"Oh dang, maybe I left it back at the office. Macy thought it would be good for the kids who are here to see you publicly apologize to Santa for your mistake in a press conference."

Beside him, Mario chuckled.

Duke had to laugh, too. He remembered that he promised Macy that he would re-create the North Pole for MJ if need be to prove to him that Santa was real. Now the scenery in his front yard made sense. It really had turned into a winter wonderland, and to make matters better, the weather had cooled down to a nice thirty degrees. The people in his front yard admiring Macy's handiwork were all dressed in sweaters and earmuffs. Macy had set up a carriage ride for those who had to park farther down the street, and even they were covered up in blankets and hand muffs.

When he got home yesterday evening, he'd found one side of his front lawn fenced in with snow and what looked like a landing strip in the center of the snow. He thought about Lawrence being a pilot and realized that he'd played a part in tonight's events. Damn, he was an ass for jumping to conclusions. Why didn't she just explain that to him? He had to find Macy.

"Serena, where is she?"

Looking innocent, Serena shrugged her shoulders. "Who?"

"Macy."

"Mom's at the office." Gia offered up the whereabouts of her mother's location as she waltzed into the room. MJ followed his sister. They paused briefly and glanced at each other before running into Duke's arms. God, he'd missed them.

"Why isn't she here?"

"I think she's still working. She wants to send that money she would have won in the Christmas decorating contest to her charity, so she's trying to figure out the books."

"But I already donated the money."

Serena snapped her fingers and pointed at him. "I knew you did it!"

He felt like such a jerk last Sunday that he'd gone down as soon as possible and written a check to the charity. Even though he'd done it anonymously, the newspaper had written up a comment in the paper yesterday and said the organization was still blessed. If Macy had seen it, she would have known that the charity still received its money, but she wouldn't have known he'd done it. "That was a secret."

"Like you bribing Andy and Spencer with football tickets?"

Duke's mouth made an O.

"Don't worry. Macy hasn't figured either out yet."

Thankful for that, Duke nodded. "So where is she?"

"Well, I don't think she's coming tonight, Duke."

"What?"

"I think she had second thoughts."

This night wasn't going to be a success without her by his side. Before taking off through the back door, Duke knelt down to Gia and MJ's level to discuss a different agenda for the night. Serena held her clipboard close and listened intently to the new plan.

He might not have had the career he had without Kristina, but he wouldn't be the man he was now without Macy. Summer, fall and now winter had passed without him investing too much time in his journalism career, but he could not stand the thought of a few days without Macy, Gia and MJ. His family. He needed her and had to have her.

It took him thirty minutes, but he finally made it to Winter Paradise. Macy's car was still in the driveway. All the lights downstairs were off, but the one in the bedroom upstairs spilled onto the steps. He pictured her in the bed under the covers, ready to shut tonight out of her mind. He wasn't about to let that happen. Tonight wouldn't have taken place if it weren't for her. She had to be a part of it.

Once he was in the foyer, he heard Macy coming down the steps. He stood still, not wanting to frighten her. "Macy," he said into the darkness.

It didn't work. She screamed the minute she saw his figure.

"It's okay. It's me, Duke," he assured her, waving his arms and crossing the room quickly so she could see his face in the light coming from upstairs. Stumbling on something on the floor, Duke met Macy on the steps. He pulled her into his arms and held her against his chest. He bet her heart was pounding from fright. His was from love.

Macy clutched her heart. "Jesus, are you trying to scare me to death?"

"I'm sorry. I just had to see you."

"How did you get in here?"

"You told me where the hideaway key is, remember?"

She glanced at the door. "And the sexy Santa? I didn't hear him go off."

Duke chuckled at her questioning and stroked her shoulders with his fingertips. He couldn't see exactly how, but he knew her hair was piled on top of her head. "Because Serena taught me how to walk by without making him talk." He pulled his head back so she could see him grin in the light.

Macy sat down on the step, still trying to catch her breath. He felt bad, he really did, but in the faint light he could see the gown Macy was wearing and felt himself harden with desire. The black material came just above her shapely thighs. Her shoulders were practically bare, and her breasts looked as if they were being served to him on a platter. The heels she wore had to be at least four inches, and her legs were encased in a dark pair of hose. As she sat down, he noticed the top of the hose and realized she was wearing garters. A week had been too long without her.

"Macy, I came over to tell you how sorry I am. I got caught up in some jealousy quicksand and couldn't get out of it."

"Jealous of what?" Macy's voice cracked.

"It doesn't matter, but what does matter is, I love you."

"You love me?" she breathed.

"Yes." He nodded. "And I'm begging you to give me one more chance." He knelt down on his knees in front of her. The last time they'd been on a set of steps, they made love for the first time. He glanced up into her dark eyes and wondered if she was remembering the same thing. "I can't take being away from you for a week. I couldn't take being away from you for a day. Hell, I already told MET I don't plan on renewing my contract."

Her mouth opened to protest. "What?"

"I turned down their offer to relocate me to a Florida station. I don't want to spend another day away from you, Macy Cuomo."

"Duke, I don't know what to say."

"Don't say anything. Just come with me to the party. You can't stay here."

She shook her head. "I didn't get this dress for nothing. What on earth made you think I wasn't?"

"Serena!" they both agreed.

Macy's cell phone rang. She reached into a little purse Duke hadn't noticed her carrying and answered it, then quickly she closed her eyes and chanted, "*I wish I'd win the lottery, I wish I'd win the lottery, I wish I'd win the lottery.*"

She'd done it before, and he had seen Serena do it, too. He watched her talk about what was going on at the house. While she was on the phone, Duke took the opportunity to caress her legs. Curiosity was getting the better of him. Her calves felt velvety beneath his hands. He couldn't believe how much he'd missed her.

It wasn't just the days that were a problem; it was just being around her. He needed her. Without her, he was nothing. He loved this woman with all his heart.

After hanging up the phone, Macy stood up and reached for the light switch just beyond Duke's head. Her breast swept across his mouth. He wondered if she'd done that on purpose. "Look, I appreciate you quitting your job, but there's more…"

Duke quieted her with a kiss. His fingers pulled her face down to his. The fog he felt that he'd been in was lifted the minutes their lips touched. His thumb caressed her cheeks. She gave him life with each kiss. When he reluctantly pulled away, he heard Macy's gasp mirror the same way he felt. Relief. They both needed that.

"Oh my God," Macy said.

Now he knew his kisses were good, but… Duke followed Macy's gaze upward. Hanging from the ceiling were dozens of sprigs of mistletoe, strategically placed where they would have no choice but to kiss all the way across the room. The walls twinkled, not with a full light, but with several hanging icicle lights, illuminating the ceiling like the night sky. The rug he thought he'd tripped on happened to be Serena's version of snow, pristine white snow.

"I love you, Macy." Duke felt the need to reiterate that under such a romantic setting. He wished to God she would say the same three words to him. But since she wasn't going to say anything just yet, he opted to kiss her again for fear of anything she had to say that he didn't want to hear. She might not have liked the idea of him sticking around more.

Her skin was like silk beneath his fingertips. The strap over her shoulder slid off with ease. A teasing moan escaped her throat as she cupped his face. His thumb touched the outer area of her nipple. Carefully, he stroked her just right. His tongued danced with hers against the beat of their hearts.

Shaking her head, Macy pulled away at the same time as she ran her hands over his chest. Her eyes were filled with tears. His heart stopped beating for a moment as she spoke.

"Duke." Macy tore her lips away from his. She shook her head. "I want to do this, I really do, but I can't be involved with you when this whole Kristina thing is still looming over us."

He mentally cursed Kristina. "Macy." He heard himself breathe her name.

"I can understand two exes being friends. Mario and I are still friends, but I would never try to pawn off another man's child on him. And I doubt he would accept anything like that."

Relieved that was the only thing wrong, Duke laughed. This was easily fixable. "I know. And I know you two are just friends. Kristina and I are not like you guys. I'll take care of her as soon as possible." Duke stood up and pulled her up with him. They moved to the bottom step and now, with her come-get-me heels on, she was a few inches shorter than him. "But I need you and the kids by my side tonight."

"At the party?"

"And after," he said with a boyish grin, then kissed

her forehead. "Let's go before I just take you upstairs and see what it is you're wearing underneath that dress."

Macy tucked her hand in his. His heart thumped faster. "Hey…" She pulled him back before they reached the door. She pointed her manicured fingertips toward the ceiling. "Are we forgetting tradition? I love you."

Duke stopped short and turned her in his arms and abided by the laws of the mistletoe. "That is the best Christmas present I've ever gotten." He dipped his head down and captured her lips.

"Just you wait until later."

Playfully, he reached for the hem of her skirt. "Does it have anything to do with what's… Ouch!" She'd popped his hand away just as his fingertips felt the promising flesh under her gown.

"Hey, I've been meaning to ask you what the deal is with you and Serena and this lottery thing."

"Oh, nothing, it's just that every time we're thinking of someone or something and then that person or thing appears, we just chant that, just in case we're granted wishes."

"So what if I say how great it would be if you kissed me?"

She rose up on her tiptoes and snaked her arms around his neck.

"Mmm, I wish I'd win the lottery…" he whispered as he pulled back and kissed her, "I wish I'd win the lottery…" he said more softly and kissed her again. "I wish I'd win the lottery. Are you ready to go?"

"Mmkay," she managed to moan.

When they reached Duke's home, the party seemed

to be in full swing. There were people from the station, people from the homes he'd helped decorate and people he'd seen in general when around town with Macy. There was nowhere to park near his house, so they parked at the end of the street and took one of Macy's carriage rides back to his front lawn. From what he could see, tons of delivery trucks were parked across his back lawn. His front yard, including the street leading up to his house, had been filled with guests' cars. The gated side with the landing strip was now filled with... As Duke looked closer, he shook his head in disbelief.

"Are those reindeer?" he asked Macy, wrapping his arms around her waist as he helped her down from the carriage. The erotic smell of her coconut shampoo made him forget he was standing in his private winter wonderland.

Macy bit her lip. "I kind of went overboard last week."

"Dare I ask how much this is going to cost me?" he teased.

Rolling her eyes, Macy slipped her hand into Duke's. There was a table on the porch with a candy-cane table-cloth. Two microphones were set up in the middle of the table with two chairs in front of them ready for the main event. They made their way over the front lawn, through the crowds and up to the bottom step of the porch. Santa came to the door, and after a lull everyone began to ooh and ahh at what was to come.

"You should probably make your apology speech." Macy nudged Duke with her elbow. She grinned when he looked down at her. "What?" She smiled innocently.

"You said you were willing to do something like this for MJ. I just figured, why not for the rest of the city?"

He didn't mind. He was on cloud nine tonight, and nothing was going to knock him off. In a mock press conference, Santa and Duke sat at a table with some of the other reporters from WKSS and discussed what a bad boy Duke had been all year long, including telling everyone Santa did not exist. Duke made his apologies for not believing in the magic of Christmas. The kids and the parents seemed to enjoy it. When the conference was over, Duke welcomed everyone to his home and thanked them for coming. He also thought this was the proper time to thank Macy, as well.

"If you all would take a moment, please welcome my better half to the floor." Duke nodded in the direction of the DJ booth at Serena. A spotlight fell across Macy's frame. She looked like a movie star. Duke held his breath and remembered the first time he'd seen her. "This whole evening wouldn't be possible if it weren't for Macy Cuomo."

The onlookers clapped and cheered Macy on to the stage. Duke opened his arm and Macy stood against him. "Macy, I just wanted to say thank you. And I can't wait to see what happens between us when the New Year rolls around." What more he wanted to say was pushed aside when he looked over and saw Kristina and their boss from DC, Oscar, climbing out of a carriage, followed by his wife, Allegra, who walked off in a different direction once her feet hit the ground.

No doubt MET had shared Duke's news with the DC station. Oscar didn't look too happy. He was middle-aged, balding and burned out from his job as a station manager. He looked even balder since the last time he'd seen him. "Thanks, everyone, for coming, and enjoy your evening," Duke said.

Everyone clapped for Duke and Santa. They all began to disperse either into the house or around the lawn. Some came up to the table and shook his hand, thanking Duke for making his apology. When they had a break, Duke took hold of Macy's hand and they walked down the steps.

"What's wrong?" Macy asked as they walked through the crowd.

"I'm about to clear the air right now," Duke replied. While more people eagerly stuck their hands out at Duke, he tried to make his way to the other side of the yard. He waited patiently and tried to greet as many people as possible, all the while keeping an eye on the folks in the back. As he approached, Mario came out of nowhere and began shaking Oscar's hand obnoxiously up and down.

Mario looked up and grinned at the sight of Duke and Macy. "Oh, great! You two made up!"

"Hi, Mario, where are the kids?" Macy said, leaning over and hugging him. Duke didn't miss the glare Macy and Kristina shot each other.

"In the house, eating." Mario pointed his beefy arm toward the home. "I have been talking a lot with my cousin, Allegra. I just came to have a word with my cousin-in-law, Oscar. Duke, you must know Oscar Orsini, right?"

"I do," Duke answered slowly. "Did you say cousin-in-law?"

"Yeah, remember when you asked if I had any Polizzi family in DC?"

"Yea?"

"Turns out in this case, I really do. My cousin Allegra."

Kristina choked on air.

"Yeah, she's married to Oscar."

Duke noticed Kristina's eyes widen. He had to laugh at the situation. Kristina, who devoured having the attention thrown on herself, cringed at the thought of Oscar's wife finding out about her. "Really?"

"Yeah, actually she's in the kitchen, so why don't you guys wait right here and I'll get her?"

"You know," Kristina said nervously, "I don't think I'm feeling very well. You guys wouldn't mind if I left early?"

"Oh, but your entourage hasn't even arrived," Macy spoke up.

Kristina offered Macy a nonapologetic smile. "Well, you know how pregnancy can be."

"Mmm, yes, I do."

"Excuse me." Gia interjected herself into the adult conversation with her phone aimed between Kristina and Duke. "This is Gia, reporting live on Snapchat from what seems like the North Pole." She focused the camera back on herself for a moment to take a selfie against the snow-covered ground before focusing back on Kristina.

Duke raised a brow at the teenager.

"Kristina," Gia continued, "congratulations on your

pregnancy. For the inquisitive kids out there watching, Duke, are you the father of Kristina's baby?"

"Absolutely not."

A few of the folks eavesdropping gasped, Macy included. She covered her mouth with one hand while trying to corral her daughter with the other. Gia stepped out of her mother's reach and followed Kristina as she tried to disappear into the crowd. "Kristina, wait, the viewers want to know who the father of your child is."

"Have you lost your mind down here?" Oscar asked, gritting his teeth. "Or has this been your plan all along, to punish me for what happened between me and Kristina?"

"Oscar, was there some reason you came tonight?" Duke asked his former boss once Kristina had left.

Clearing his throat, Oscar nodded. "There was. I wanted to talk to you about your contract. You know I can sue you."

"For what? My contract is with MET, who set me up at your station. Might I remind you that you were the one who signed off on my leave of absence? Go ahead, Oscar."

"I don't think he's going to sue you." Mario draped his arm over the shorter man's shoulder. "Are you, *cugino*? I think we ought to go into the kitchen. I know Allegra doesn't like to be kept waiting." As he walked by Duke and Macy, he winked at them.

"Wow. What an evening," Macy said, sinking against him.

"Do you think you'll miss all this excitement when I'm no longer in the limelight?" Duke whispered in her ear.

"Is that your little dig on Tallahassee news not being so big?"

There was just something about the way she looked at him. It made Duke's heart swell. Her hair was piled up on top of her head with a few curls hanging down framing her face. "No, I meant now that I'm not going to make as much money, seeing how the local high school coaches don't make much."

"High school coach?"

Duke took Macy in his arms. "Yeah, you see, a little birdie told me that there was a high school baseball coach position open, and I was offered the job and I took it."

When her face lit up, he smiled. "Seriously?"

"Very much so. And I have to say that this last week has made me realize that my life is nothing without you."

Macy pushed away and folded her arms across her chest. "Nothing?" she squeaked out.

"Nothing," Duke repeated, enjoying the look of disbelief on her face. Gia returned from the crowd with MJ in tow. They flanked Duke. "I am more than willing to give up the fame and fortune just to be with you." Taking a deep breath, he got down on one knee.

Macy covered her face. "What are you doing?"

"Well, I asked the kids earlier and they agreed to have me. And now I would like to ask you to marry me."

"Oh my God!"

"Macy Cuomo, a week without you was the most torturous ever. I don't ever want to spend any more time away from you. Will you please marry me?" He realized the crowd behind him had quieted down and had begun paying attention to them.

"Well?" shouted someone from the crowd. Duke was pretty sure it was Serena's voice.

"Yes!" Macy cried.

Duke stood up and spun Macy around in his arms. "You just don't know how happy you've made me. I only wish my parents were here to meet you!"

Macy buried her face against his neck. He could feel her warm breath against his collarbone. "Duke, listen, that thing I was working with Lawrence on."

"It doesn't matter…"

"It kind of does." She wiggled out of his arms and slid down to her feet. "There's what we were working on."

Duke followed her bare finger toward the street where a long stretch limousine had pulled up. A chauffeur ran around from the driver's side to the back door and opened it. He did a double take at the sight of what he thought he saw.

"Ma?" The word escaped him as the emotions caught in his throat. His mother had stepped out of the backseat, followed by his father, his two sisters, Ana and Theresa, and then his brothers, Erik, Bobby and Sandino. Duke looked back down at Macy by his side. She was tearfully looking up at him.

"I didn't want to tell you what Lawrence and I were working on last week because I wanted this to be a surprise."

"How did you—"

"Pablo and Monique helped coordinate. Lawrence flew his plane and picked them up earlier this evening."

"Macy, I don't know what to say…"

"How about you just introduce me to my new family?"

A stroke after midnight, Macy stood on the porch, waving away Duke's last guest. He had gone inside to say good-night to his family and met her in the foyer. Macy closed the door behind her and held on to the doorknob. Duke was standing at the bottom of his steps.

"We have to stop meeting like this," she teased, cocking her eyebrow toward the steps. He looked breathtakingly handsome with his button-down Oxford shirt rolled up to his elbows.

"I don't think I'm ever going to look at stairs the same way," Duke said, walking up on her. His hands pressed against the door on either side of her head. "You know, I fell in love with you in front of the Baezes' stairs. You were standing right under the same mistletoe." He nodded toward the ceiling, encouraging her eyes to follow where he hung the dried plant.

"You did not." She beamed inwardly, but held her composure. "This is the same one?"

"*Es verdad.*"

She smiled. "I already agreed to marry you. You don't have to woo me with your tricks."

"Okay, *mi future esposa.*"

Macy closed her eyes and moaned, "We are not going to do anything with your parents in the other room."

"I'll be quiet."

"Yes, but I might not be." Macy giggled. "Hey, speaking of your parents, you know you didn't close your eyes and wish to win the lottery when you saw them."

He dipped his head down and inhaled a kiss. "That's because I already have, Macy. I already have won. Thanks to you and the children, I have my own family."

* * * * *

Everyone in the room turned at the same time.
Gianna Martelli stood in the doorway, a bright smile
painting her expression. Donovan pushed himself up
from his seat, a wave of anxiety washing over him.
Gianna met his stare, a nervous twitch pulsing at the edge
of her lip. Light danced in her eyes as her gaze shifted
from the top of his head to the floor beneath his feet and
back, finally setting on his face.

Donovan Boudreaux was neatly attired, wearing a
casual summer suit in tan-colored linen with a white dress
shirt open at the collar. Brown leather loafers completed
his look. His dark hair was cropped low and close, and
he sported just the faintest hint of a goatee. His features
were chiseled, and at first glance she could have easily
mistaken him for a high fashion model. Nothing about

him screamed teacher. The man was drop-dead gorgeous, and as she stared, he took her breath away.

The moment was suddenly surreal, as though everything was moving in slow motion. As she glided to his side, Donovan was awed by the sheer magnitude of the moment, feeling as if he was lost somewhere deep in the sweetest dream. And then she touched him, her slender arms reaching around to give him a warm hug.

"It's nice to finally meet you," Gianna said softly. "Welcome to Italy."

Donovan's smile spread full across his face, his gaze dancing over her features. Although she and her sister were identical, he would have easily proclaimed Gianna the most beautiful woman he'd ever laid eyes on. The photo on the dust jacket of her books didn't begin to do her justice. Her complexion was dark honey, a sun-kissed glow emanating from unblemished skin. Her eyes were large saucers, blue-black in color, and reminded him of vast expanses of black ice. Her features were delicate, a button nose and thin lips framed by lush, thick waves of jet-black hair that fell to midwaist on a petite frame. She was tiny, almost fragile, but carried herself as though she stood inches taller. She wore a floral-print, ankle-length skirt and a simple white shirt that stopped just below her full bustline, exposing a washboard stomach. Gianna Martelli was stunning!

Don't miss
TUSCAN HEAT by Deborah Fletcher Mello,
available January 2016 wherever
Harlequin® Kimani Romance™
books and ebooks are sold.